Ohio Angels

by

Harriet Scott Chessman

THE PERMANENT PRESS
SAG HARBOR, NY 11963

Library of Congress Cataloging-in-Publication Data

Harriet Scott Chessman
 Ohio Angels / by Harriet Scott Chessman
  p. cm.
 ISBN 1-57962-020-5
 I. Title.
 PS3553.H4225O35 1999
 813'.54--dc21   98-34208
              CIP

THE PERMANENT PRESS
4170 Noyac Road
Sag Harbor, NY 11963

To
Eleanor Osgood Chessman and George Wallace Chessman,
with love

Contents

the bone-frame was made for
no such shock knit within terror,
yet the skeleton stood up to it:

the flesh? it was melted away,
the heart burnt out, dead ember,
tendons, muscles shattered, outer husk dismembered,

yet the frame held:
we passed the flame: we wonder
what saved us? what for?

H.D., "The Walls Do Not Fall," in *Trilogy*

I. Hallie

Her mother's bedroom seemed to float in light, so sunny that Hallie blinked as she entered. Her mother lay on top of the bed in a slip, her head on a mound of pillows, her eyes closed. On the bedtable sat an alarm clock and books.

Hallie walked softly toward the bed, hesitating as she got closer.

Her mother opened her eyes.

"Hi, Mom." Hallie looked around to see where to sit. The blue plush armchairs sat at the other side of the room. "How are you?"

"Dandy." Her mother's mouth bent into a kind of smile.

Hallie lowered herself gingerly to the end of the bed.

For a moment her mother looked like a girl, polite and full of compunction.

"It was sweet of you to come all this way."

"I wanted to. I thought I could help."

Her mother looked at her.

"Help? Why? Did your father tell you I needed help?"

"Well." Hallie felt uncomfortable. "He said you've stayed in bed for almost a month."

"What does he know? He isn't even here half the time. I get out of bed. I got out this morning."

Hallie could not think what to say. She looked at the white carpet, shining in the sun. Her mother had so much more space than she and Morey had in Brooklyn, although Hallie liked their new apartment. All down the block, young trees had been planted, and if you bent close to the front windows you could see the edges of a little park. Outside her mother's windows, Hallie knew, lay the two lawn terraces and the pool, and a wash of green spilling down the hill. In winter, you could look through the trees to see the valley, tiny farmhouses like white punctuation marks on larger sheets of ash, sepia, gold, with the roads winding gray and sometimes silver across the landscape.

She gazed at her mother's face, a map of tiny wrinkles, but with the same high cheekbones, the same broad fore-head. Her hair looked thin now, with only touches of blonde in the gray. Her mother had closed her eyes again, and Hallie studied the faint blue color of her eyelids. It reminded her of the forget-me-nots in Rose's garden. She and Rose used to pick them and put them in orange juice glasses on the counter for Rose's mother.

Hallie thought about how shy her father had looked this morning at the airport, waving to Hallie over the crowd of people. Hal, he had said, bending to kiss her. Awkward, she had bent to smooth her skirt, but outside, walking to the car, her heart had thrilled at the familiar scent of oil and hay, the green flatness and the humid breeze.

In the car as it ambled past new developments and fields of corn and wheat, Hallie had remembered riding with her father on errands. His solidity had been quiet and contemplative, his foot on the pedal urging the car forward, to the airport sometimes to pick up Grandmother Holloway, or an aunt or uncle, who would step off the plane looking dressed up, odd, not like an Ohioan at all, and they would keep this formal shine, in the design of their clothes and the way they held themselves, until she and her father drove them back, and Hallie would sit proudly in the front, feeling at home.

How's your painting? her father had asked in the car, glancing at Hallie, a look of uncertainty on his face. When she had told him about the oils she'd done last year, he had gazed at the sky for a moment, his hands clutching the wheel, and asked, Now, do you have people in them, or landscapes, or are you still making them kind of abstract?

Sitting on her mother's bed in the early afternoon light, she thought of those canvases, with pencilled arrows and angles, compass points, sketched on top of delicately modelled white and gray, aerial views of a wilderness, filled with mountains that, from the air, looked small, barely perceptible. She had begun with earth tones, but gradually she'd turned to white and shades of gray, sometimes a speck of red, so surprising in the expanse that it had the impact of a sudden moment of violence, or passion. Each one had "Map" in the title, for they were maps, maybe of the heart, more than of any actual place, and of the body too. She'd been proud of those, and two had sold.

This spring, though, she'd come to an impasse. She'd attempted to move on to something new, but she hadn't been happy with any of her sketches. She hadn't even felt able to begin stretching a new canvas. She would stare out the window of her studio, studying the gray building opposite, and the cars below, the pigeons roosting on lintels and jutting sills, the changing sky. She'd look for any excuse to wrap things up and turn off the light, walking the five stories down to the street.

"How's Morey?" Her mother's blue eyes looked amused and bitter.

"He's fine."

"He didn't feel like coming to Ohio?" Her mother emphasized each syllable of "Ohio."

"He's really busy." Hallie tried to look open, as if her mother's questions were simple. She added, "His firm has a new commission, for a big project on Long Island."

"Oh?" Her mother looked at Hallie as if she might say something about Morey or architects, or big projects on Long Island. Hallie stood up and looked out the window. A wheelbarrow, filled with weeds, sat by one of the beds, and a hand-rake lay on the walk.

"Who's been gardening?"

Her mother used to hire a local college student to do the gardening, in the spring and fall. In the summer, the garden spilled over its bounds and straggled. Hallie had always been relieved to see a new student each September, kneeling on the stone walkway, pulling out armfuls of weeds, pinching off the heads of marigolds and cutting back the phlox, their leaves whitish from summer blight.

Her mother laughed a dry laugh. "Your father's become a gardener. Although I doubt that he knows what he's doing."

Hallie looked at the flower bed. Someone had planted a cheerful bunch of lavender and white flowers along the border.

"It looks like he's doing a good job," she said, and her mother gave a soft snort.

13

As she looked at her father's gardening gloves, abandoned by the side of the pool, Hallie thought about how puzzled and sad Morey had looked this morning at breakfast, sitting at the counter in his old t-shirt and jeans. She missed him now. As soon as she was away from him, she missed him. At home, though, things he did could touch off a fury inside her. She could be having a difficult time with him, arguing about something, and as soon as the phone rang, he'd be genial, laughing and making jokes. Often he'd miss dinner without warning, and come home from work around ten or eleven at night. He had become so busy that they hadn't left the city once this summer.

In other summers, on good days, they had sometimes packed up the car to find a beach near a small town. Hallie would sketch or work in her notebook, and Morey would read the paper. Sometimes he would lie on his back with the newspaper over his head, like an old man, and fall asleep, while Hallie studied the horizon and wondered what it would be like to catch the breezes on a sailboat.

Hallie looked at her mother's face on the white pillows. She found herself thinking about Morey, how she'd first loved him because he believed in painting as something important in the world. His father had been a painter, although he had never become well-known, and Morey had told her how, growing up, he had watched the way a canvas takes on color and shape. Morey had admired her work, and at first she had wished him to see each new painting from conception on, yet somehow she had begun to keep her new work to herself. She had discovered that the smallest amount of criticism from him, even a pause, could send her into a period of terrible doubt, when she felt compelled to put turpentine on a rag and rub out all of her new strokes by the end of each day.

Her mother picked up the alarm clock and began to wind it.

"You know, Rose lives in town now. She moved here a few years ago, right back to the house on Broadway."

"I know." How can Rose live here, thought Hallie, so far from an ocean? An image came to her, of Rose opening and closing her mouth for breath in the moist Ohio air, but she rubbed it out, thinking, Rose is different from me. A place changes depending on who's looking at it.

Coming into town this morning with her father, Hallie had thought, with surprise, how thriving and substantial this is. In her memory, the houses had a somber cast, an untended look. This town looked polished, even wealthy. The large rectangles and squares of old houses looked imposing, a bright white, as on a New England green. Perhaps her memories had begun to resemble photographs from her childhood, black and white, with sharply cut figures squeezed between four lines. How funny to have to discover that a place had its own life, outside of photographs or memories: this boy here, skateboarding, or that plump tabby cat on the porch, asleep under baskets spilling flowers—oh! Hallie had thought, that's Rose's house, and as the car rolled on she had turned to look again at Rose's wide, calm porch fronting Broadway. Quickly, she had looked to the other side of the street, to see the open space where her first house used to be. She could not remember when the house had been torn down. It must have been a long time after they moved, because she used to stand on Rose's porch afterwards, looking across Broadway to see her old house's humble shape. She had been seven when the walls had become suddenly bare, as chairs and beds made a parade outside to the moving van. Magnificent trees, thick and arching, still stood, shading the lawn, and for one moment Hallie thought she could see the house again in its natural space, with its white face to the street.

Hallie glanced at her mother. She looked as if she might be asleep. What had they been talking about? She gazed at the curtains and at the sky, now a pale blue, the sun whitened. Rose, she thought, Rose of the thick red hair, so different from her own thin brown hair cut in an airy bowl around her face. Rose's hair had had a will of its own. Sometimes Rose's mother had pulled it into a French braid or knot, but most of the time she had let Rose brush it back to be caught in a thick bee-swarm.

Broadway had been the river to be negotiated. You had

to be careful, crossing, and wait on the island in the middle until all of the cars and trucks were out of sight, but even at five Hallie had crossed on her own. Rose had created a system of signals: a white washcloth waving from Rose's porch meant come over, and a red cloth, waved up and down, meant come in ten minutes, or in circles over your head meant I can't play now, and blue meant—what had blue meant? Hallie couldn't remember.

"You know she's pregnant again."

Hallie hugged her elbows. She looked her mother full in the face, daring her to say more.

"I saw her downtown a month ago, as big as a church, with her daughters. The youngest one—what's her name?"

"Sophie."

"Sophie was throwing a tantrum on the sidewalk."

Hallie shrugged, and saw again in her mind's eye the streaks of brown blood heralding her fifth, and last, miscarriage. That evening, she had sat in the bathroom of the restaurant as the blood came in earnest, against all of her inner commands to her uterus to hold out and keep what could still, miraculously, become a baby. The thick clots of blood, dark red, had seemed to Hallie, against all knowledge, signs of her own insufficiency. She had only pretended to be an ordinary woman, with a whole and satisfactory body.

"I'll just do a little unpacking." Hallie carried her bag down the wide hall into her old room at the front of the house.

The bed was high but small. Hallie thought of her grandmother, Sarah Holloway, who had given her the white cover with tiny blue flowers embroidered along the edges. She had seen her grandmother as formidable, a quietly strong-willed woman, not particularly warm or easy to talk to. She had been born and raised in Virginia, and had lived all her married life in Philadelphia. For days before Grandmother Holloway's annual visit, Hallie's mother would clean the house as if she were another woman, dusting bookshelves and clearing off each surface until the house had a starched look Hallie loved. During

Grandmother Holloway's stay the family would eat together in the dining room, on her mother's wedding china, instead of at the kitchen table with paper napkins and regular dishes. Grandmother Holloway asked for water with her lunch, an elegant austerity Hallie had held in awe.

Hallie missed the mother who could bring her small family together at the table. Sometimes, on a magical Sunday, even when Grandmother Holloway was not there, Hallie's mother would rise out of bed and decide to make chicken fried the way her old cook had taught her. Hallie would help her flour the thighs and breasts and watch as her mother placed the pieces in the pan, sizzling in oil. Her mother seemed to her at such times a lovely woman, confident in her movements, and Hallie stood close to her, as if such beauty could shine on her and protect her always.

Most Sundays were different, but so habitual that Hallie thought nothing of them. One Sunday morning, in the old house, Rose had come over and Hallie had helped her make a sandwich. Where's your mother? Rose had asked. Asleep, said Hallie. Is she sick? No, and suddenly Hallie had had a new thought. Other children's mothers did not sleep all morning and deep into the afternoon. She remembered with amazement how Rose's mother was always awake, and how she made sandwiches, cutting them into triangles on white plates and placing them on the table, and she felt ashamed.

"Charles!" Hallie could hear her mother calling. She got up and opened her door just enough to see her mother standing in her slip at the top of the stairs.

"Charles! Where is he?" and she looked lost, like a child who cannot find its mother in the middle of the night because the house's darkness is too thick between them.

Hallie waited until she heard her mother move back to bed. Her father started up the mower outside, and she wondered if his feet were bare, as they always used to be. Wild cherries, rotting on the second lawn terrace, above the pool, would stain his toes and sometimes he would stub a toe on a stone and shout "Damn!" Once he stepped on a bee, and

17

Hallie remembered how his foot had swollen like a water bottle and how he had had to go down to his office and ask his nurse, pretty Mary Helen Hennessey, who always gave her a lifesaver, to give him a shot.

She slipped into the hallway. The large mirror, with bevelled edges that made a rainbow, held the light. She went into the study, across from her room, and sat at the cherry writing desk with the cubbyholes and the slanting lid. The phone sat, stolidly, black with a circular dial, the same one that had always been here. Hallie put her finger into one of the circles and moved the dial, letting it go to hear the clickety whirr. Her father's medical school books, fat textbooks with long Latinate names in gold letters, sat on the bottom shelves. As a child, she had tiptoed in here sometimes to open them, breathing in the smell of old paper and contemplating the tiny print and little diagrams with letters—"a," "b," "c," "f," "z"—pointing to organs or blood vessels, bones or layers of flesh.

Opening the phone book, she thought, Rose, Rose, and paused. Good heavens, what was her last name now? Banford, it had been, but William's name was (Hallie tapped a pencil on the cherry desk and looked out the window, surprised to see a hummingbird at the edge of the front lawn) Haas. I haven't seen Rose for years now, thought Hallie, remembering how Rose and William had come to New York for a couple of days one June. Rose had been pregnant with her first child then, her huge belly almost disturbing to Hallie. Hallie owned only a handful of photographs of Rose, two of them from that visit. In one, Rose was sitting at the kitchen counter in the old loft, her blue flowered dress sleeveless, her arms plump. She leaned toward William, laughing, her mouth stuffed with cake and her fingers covered with yellow frosting, like pollen. In another, Rose stood next to the big window, her arms folded over her belly. She looked straight at the camera with a wry, half-smiling, questioning gaze.

As a child, Hallie had admired Rose's superior knowledge of the world. Rose had known all about babies, and about the astonishing ovaries curled inside Hallie's and Rose's slender bodies, and the regal Fallopian tubes holding open passageways for the eggs that would one day emerge, and the sturdy uteruses, strong as Rose's fist when she shook it in anger. Rose would trace her finger along Hallie's belly, showing the position of each tight organ, as if she had the power to see through Hallie's skin, into the bowl of her future. Rose's house had been filled with babies—two came after Rose—and with information too. You could ask Rose's mother anything, Hallie thought, and she would not look shocked. Not that Hallie ventured such questions, but she saw how to make discoveries by just keeping her ears open when Rose or her older sister Catherine made inquiries.

For years, in fact, Hallie had believed that such information could only come in the form of an English accent, the Banfords having come to Ohio from England when Rose was four. Hallie had loved to hear Rose's mother speak, her voice gentle and odd. She's from Bath, Rose had told her, only she calls it Bahth. Bath? Hallie had asked doubtfully, amazed that a whole town could be named for something so small and ordinary. An improbable transplanting, Hallie mused now, as she looked up the H's in the phone book and saw Haas, Rose and William, 200 Broadway. Rose's father had been handsome, with hair over his forehead and a quick smile. He had been the editor of the newspaper in the bigger town nearby, a position that had seemed vaguely royal to Hallie. He wrote poetry, too, and two slender books of his poems sat right on the shelf of the Banfords' living room. All this was unusual in Hallie's world. Her mother and father read books, but she had never known someone who wrote them. She had tried to read his poems once, when she was about ten, and she remembered a lot of descriptions of trees, and one phrase: "you branch and flower."

Have an egg? he had asked her once at breakfast at Rose's house, his hair uncombed, his eyes bright, as if cut with light. Oh, yes, she had said, please, and she had blushed as he got her an egg cup and tapped the egg open for her, the insides yellow and smooth and wet, his fingers quick, scooping out the small bit of the egg's hat and offering it to her in the spoon. He had married again after Mrs. Banford's death, she had heard, a much younger woman, and Rose had written to her two years ago to say that he had died.

It was Mrs. Banford, Hallie thought, who had told her stories about fairies—not fairy tales, but stories about tiny creatures with wings, who might tip the spoon out of your cereal bowl or make your hair look as if you'd been rolling around in hay, or bring you good dreams on a moonlit night. And Rose had had a gift for knowing how fairies could be lured into little houses made of bricks and stones, filled with miniature chairs and tables and beds, with bits of dandelions and purple myrtle flowers left inside as offerings. Rose and Hallie would become absorbed for hours, on long summer days in the Banfords' garden, creating houses for these small folk. Was it a propitiation, Hallie wondered now (she picked up the receiver and began to dial), and why did fairies need to be propitiated? What would a fairy do if you did not feed it raspberry jam on tiny crackers? Or was the idea to make the fairies comfortable, to give them a home and a place to rest, when so many people gave them no thought at all?

"Hello?"

Hallie's throat felt suddenly thick. "Rose?" she asked.

The mower droned to a halt, and as Hallie hesitated, she saw her father, in his sandals, walk across the front yard. He bent toward the mailbox, and, opening it, peered inside, pulling out a bundle of envelopes and catalogues.

II. Rose

At five Saturday morning Rose woke to a mighty activity in her uterus. Small feet pummelled her from the inside, pushing out as if to create an opening in her belly and greet daybreak. She held her hand over the pummellings, just under her breast, and then she pushed gently in. For a moment she felt a lull and contemplated the gold sunlight making patterns on the wood floor of the bedroom. This gold and these patterns, this sensation of lull and anticipation, had filled her mornings the summer of Elizabeth's birth. Elizabeth had been delicate as a baby. Her high cries had floated down the hallway, urging Rose's milk to flow in thin bluish streams down her belly and, as she arose, onto the floor. Early morning had never before seemed so full of scents and beauty. The smallest objects—a cup and saucer on her dresser, the baby's yellow shirt, the fine white powder on the changing table—all took on a distinctness, an importance, as if to say, Take note of us, this is the texture of your life, this is not metaphor but the thing itself.

Metaphor lured Rose always. It had begun to seem to her a miracle, an impossibility (the strenuous yoking of two unlike things together), a wild and fertile instance of marriage, that changes the world. The rolling landscape of my belly, that is a metaphor. The house, the embrace, and here Rose felt huge turnings inside, as if the baby had begun a wild dance of somersaults. She tried to think of another figure, but the baby made its presence known as something outside metaphor, too astonishing for description. Whatness, she thought. Metaphor lures me, but I am ravished by whatness too.

Rose moved onto her side and closed her eyes, trying to go back to sleep, but the world inside her came exuberantly awake. Her belly felt as if two or three fat melons were rolling up and under each other, bulging out in surprising directions. How is it possible to contain this baby, this new person, inside my own body? thought Rose sleepily. How can it be so content in my uterus, and know nothing of the world outside?—of William sleeping here, or sunlight, or even me, really?—although of course this baby knows me in another way. It knows how my blood rushes, how my voice sounds, sifting through layers of skin and organs. Maybe you can never know another person better. To be inside another, to have another inside. How to understand this?

William moved in his sleep onto his back, his breath quiet and regular. Rose studied his straight fair hair, his brown skin, the fine stubble on his cheek. He looked sober and vulnerable, without his daytime quickness. She had an urge to kiss him. But I should let him sleep, she thought, remembering how he had been up around two in the morning. She had woken to the sound of a cat on the front lawn, a disturbing drawn-out cry of all the vowels at once, and she had seen the outline of his pillow, the dark space where his body would have glimmered. As she walked to the hall bathroom, she had seen a light on downstairs, and she had found him in the kitchen, standing by the sink and washing out a cup. You can't sleep? she had asked, rubbing her eyes. The cat had yowled again, and William had opened the door to the porch, calling softly to their little cat Mitzi, but Mitzi did not come. I was thinking about my book, he had said, as he turned off the porch light and put the cup away. Rose had pressed her head against his back. It's two o'clock in the morning, she had said, it's just one night in the middle of a summer in the middle of Ohio, and William had leaned into her. They had stood that way for a long time, until Rose had said, Come to bed.

Rose saw herself in the mirror of the dressing table, and caught sadness on her face. Her breasts looked pendulous beneath her nightgown, and her eyes looked clouded and gray, not green. Her red hair, streaked with silver and in a shock of curls around her face, looked as if she had been tearing at it in sorrow and anguish. But I haven't, she thought, and how am I sad with such a splendid belly, bigger than a kettle, a beach ball (she stood up and stretched), a Japanese lantern.

But I am tired, thought Rose. She remembered how,

during her first pregnancy, all the world had seemed to become riper and slower. On weekends or in the evenings William sometimes would bring her lemonade or tea, and she would drink with her feet on his lap. Once children have popped out and begun to grow up, she thought, you plunge into life in a whole new way. William was so much more preoccupied with his teaching, and his book, and so often he seemed restless, discontented. And here was Sophie, who seemed troubled these days, waking in the middle of the night with bad dreams. How could Rose help her? She would have a talk with her, and ask what was on her mind. Maybe she's worried about my going to the hospital, thought Rose. Only five more weeks. Maybe she thinks she'll lose me.

Rose brushed her hair. She wrapped William's green robe over her nightgown and walked into the wide hallway and down the stairs with the curving banister. Opening the kitchen door for Mitzi, she thought with sudden remembrance, today Hallie comes. Rose had become so used to being accompanied by the memory of Hallie, especially now that she lived in this house again, that it was difficult to believe she could actually see her. Hallie, above all other childhood friends, seemed still to be present, eating sandwiches on the back steps, drawing pictures in Rose's old bedroom, the square one in the front of the house that Elizabeth and Sophie now shared. Rose bent to pour milk for the cat into a chipped blue plate. The house seemed for a moment to hold all of Rose's history simultaneously. A five-year-old Hallie could walk into the kitchen from the garden as easily as the five-year-old Sophie would call down to her in (here Rose looked at the kitchen clock, to see the small hand near six and the long one climbing to the top) another hour. And Rose's mother could sit reading the paper at the kitchen table (Rose glanced at the chair across from her) even though she had been dead for seventeen years.

The clock ticked, and Mitzi bent her head in miniature grace to clean her paws. A truck changed gears on

Broadway, and a car whirred by. Rose listened to someone clattering plates in the house next door. The most difficult thing, she thought, is this: how can you be sure even of what appears closest and most ordinary to you? Even when someone lives and breathes near you, can you know them from the inside, can you know what they wish to hide, or what they don't even know about themselves? Is my mother (was my mother, she corrected herself) the woman I saw? Or is she another country, one that I can read about in books and even visit, but in whom I am a tourist, a foreigner? Or Hallie.

As Rose sponged the kitchen counter, she remembered a splendid night, about this time of year, oh, it must have been thirty years ago. She had been lying on a blanket with Hallie near the big beech tree at the back of the garden as the shadows lengthened and the sky became orange and then dusky red, the leaves sharp-edged in the upper air, until the trees turned a deep purple against a purple sky and the stars began to shine. Around the children, fireflies blinked, searching the hedges and branches, and the peepers made summer noises. Rose's mother came out to tell them to fold up the blanket and come in, but when they begged her for more time, she sighed and lay down next to them. Soon she began to tell stories about the stars, so that the sky became a book created out of light. After one story about two little cats who fooled a cruel magician into making himself into stars, Hallie's voice had floated out of the darkness, Is that true? and Rose's mother had laughed, Of course, and Hallie had said, No, but really? and Rose's mother had said, It can be true if you like to think it's true, and Hallie had said, I do.

Another day Hallie had surprised Rose by saying she did not know what an angel looked like, and Rose, who as a child thought about angels as easily as she thought about breakfast, had said, as she sat with Hallie halfway up the stairs in the front hallway, Oh, well, of course they are quite big. Big? Hallie had asked, looking at once skeptical and anxious. Yes, as big as a grown-up, Rose had said, and with huge wings too, made of feathers. I thought angels were tiny, Hallie had said, and when Rose had said Oh no, Hallie had stood up and said, I'm glad I haven't seen one then.

Rose poured milk into a bowl of cereal and rummaged for a spoon. Angels were not so easy to come by, certainly not the ones she had told Hallie about, floating above the trees at dusk or standing at the top of the stair to deliver a message. On the other hand (here Rose opened the screen door with her foot and walked onto the back porch to see a fine mist hovering in the middle distance of the garden, among the hollyhocks and the sprays of lavender), on the other hand, who could say about angels? Maybe you could only sense their presence indirectly—in laundry, or holly-hocks. And what would their message be? she thought as she ate her cereal and watched the sun turn the top of the beech tree into gold.

Rose thought she heard someone laughing in the gar-den. She looked, and saw her father, a vivid and elegant man, leaning on the grass, narrowing his eyes, and laugh-ing, as if he found her thoughts delightfully funny. Why should you laugh about angels? she asked him. You're making fun of me. Not so, he said, Rose of my life, I'm just a doubting sort. Hmph, Rose said. And she would have said more, but the baby—the porpoise—sent slow waves down her belly. Rose shifted in her porch chair, and when she looked again she saw only the garden in need of tending.

Soon a high voice called to her, and the day began anew as Rose gathered herself to climb the stairs and greet Sophie, who was sitting up in the double bed. Elizabeth's red hair lay spread over her pillow, and her breath came evenly. Rose put her finger to her lips and Sophie jumped lightly out of bed and ran on tiptoes to the stairs.

"Elizabeth snores," said Sophie as she hopped from step to step.

"Oh my."

"And she talks in her sleep."

"What does she say?"

Sophie thought. She held her toe in the air above the last step. "'Help.' She says 'Help' and 'Go away.'"

"Hm. I wonder what she's dreaming about, Sophie?"

"Probably a crocodile. Probably a crocodile's chasing her and she's in a river. If she yells 'Help' someone will save her."

"Who would that be?"

"Oh, probably me." Sophie danced into the kitchen to choose a box of cereal. Her hair made a fuzzy cloud around her head as she poured the milk slowly.

"Yes, you're a brave one, Sophie."

A look of contentment settled on Sophie's face. "I can fight a crocodile."

Fierce child, thought Rose, pugnacious one, making light of crocodiles. I will make something out of that, and soon, soon (Rose glanced at the clock; only seven o'clock; William still slept). How will it go? Rose mused, feeling full with the idea of Sophie and longing for a white sheet of paper, ready for the shape of the story. She saw Sophie in a book, battling a crocodile, her soft hair flying. And will they become friends, she wondered, envisioning a final spread of the two figures with their arms about each other, grinning, their party hats lopsided.

Such a good book that could be, mused Rose, spooning tea into her mother's teapot and pouring in the water. The fine dark pieces swirled in a fragrant dance beneath the steam. She imagined a shelf filled with the books she had written, bright thin picture books with comical illustrations a child would love. "Sophie and the Crocodile," she murmured. She might write this one, as she had written the others, but who knew when someone would say yes to one, and make it into something tangible, with shiny covers and dedications? To William, one would say. To Sophia and Elizabeth. To the memory of my mother. Writing was a gift, held out to another: Here you are, she could imagine saying. This is for you. I wrote it because of you. You are in it, mingling with the words and the pictures and the scent of the page. In her father's first book of poems, the dedication said To Claire, with deepest love. And in the second, the dedication said To Catherine, Rose, Hannah, and Jacob. Rose had often opened the book to that page, to wonder at her name in print.

Her mother had had the gift of story-telling, holding this gift as casually as she held a trowel or a hairbrush, as if she might say, Oh yes, well, here's another one. She never seemed to think about actually writing any of her stories down. Catherine and Rose asked for a new one each night as they punched their pillows and drew the sheets up to their chins, and their mother would look at the floor for a moment, or at the lamp, and then begin. Often the stories were like chapters in a book; Rose could remember two characters, Shiner and Hallelujah, who resembled Catherine and herself, and who had adventures night after night, climbing mountains to find stars, and capturing pirates, and riding in balloons to China.

Stirring a teaspoon of sugar into her tea, Rose thought about the photographs Hallie had sent her of her most recent paintings, with words and arrows in pencil on top of swaths of white. They were handsome, cool in tone, offering just enough hints to make you gaze for a long time, as if you could discover something carefully folded into the paint. Hallie had become elegant, Rose thought, as she contemplated the places on William's bathrobe where the buttons had fallen off, and her toes, freckled and blunt-edged. How would Hallie look at her now? I've grown slower and fatter with each year, my hair grayer and more brittle. Rose Haas, would-be writer, plump woman, plumped down in the middle of the slow state of Ohio.

"How many Cheerios can fit on a spoon?" Sophie asked.

"How big is the spoon?"

"This spoon, silly." Sophie waved her teaspoon.

Rose thought. "I'd say twelve."

Sophie carefully plucked soggy Cheerios out of the milk to put on her spoon. "Ten, eleven, twelve . . . thirteen! Fourteen! Fourteen, you were wrong."

Rose smiled and smoothed Sophie's hair. Helping her to a second bowl, Rose thought of the new writing that had come to her out of the humid air this summer. The characters had come first, one after another, asking her to listen, and she had begun, gingerly at first, to try out a couple of pages at a time, seeing how each one spoke. This would not be for children (children must be protected, she thought), but for grown-ups—that funny word—people who know something about disappointment. And don't children know about disappointment, she asked herself, listening to Sophie hum as she ate. Yes, but stories for children are hopeful, and often comical too. Some of the characters talking to her as she watered the garden and got dressed in the morning were hopeful, but their situations were intricate, a happy ending difficult to find. The character Rose most loved was a figure like her mother.

Washing the last dish and putting it on the rack to dry, Rose felt a fullness in the space behind her right elbow, and imagined her mother standing there, listening to Rose's thoughts and wishing to speak. She looked over her shoulder to see air, and Sophie drinking the milk from her bowl on the floor.

"I'm a mountain lion," said Sophie, "and I'm about to go hunting. I'm drinking from the lake."

Rose felt tired. She sat down, frowning at Sophie, and put her feet up on a chair. Water rushed through the pipes, and Rose said, "I think Daddy's up." Sophie ran out of the kitchen, her nightgown billowing around her.

Soon Rose heard Sophie jumping on a bed, as William raised his voice to order her off, and Elizabeth shouted that she couldn't find any underwear. After awhile Sophie came into the kitchen to announce, "We're going out to breakfast at Luke's with Daddy, and I'm ordering pancakes," and Rose thought Ah, maybe I'll have a space of quiet for an hour.

Rose walked out to the hall. William came downstairs with wet hair and opened the door, and Rose stepped onto the front porch in her bare feet.

"Would you like to come?" he asked, as the girls jumped from the porch to the lawn, urging him to come quickly. "We'll wait for you."

"I might just stay here," said Rose.

"We could drive if the walk seems too big."

Rose thought of the cheerfulness of Luke's, and how the girls would choose songs in the jukeboxes, and how she would order something sweet and sticky, with a cup of coffee. She had always loved breakfasts with William.

"O.K. I'll come, but you go ahead. Let me just jump into the shower, and I'll meet up with you."

"I'll take them to the drugstore first," said William. Elizabeth and Sophie called to him from halfway down the block, and he called, "Wait up."

William jogged down the walk, and then sauntered, wet hair glistening, hands in his pockets. Rose remembered how he'd looked the first summer she'd known him, when she had come home, after her second year of graduate school, once her father had married the absurdly young and shy and big-breasted Laura and moved to Pennsylvania. I'm thinking of selling the house, her father had told her. No, no, she had said, let me come and live in it, I can go back up for my orals, and I can use the college library for my dissertation. Catherine had been astonished, and so had Hallie. But the house took her in, embraced her, and made a calm place for her, utterly unlike her tiny apartment in Ann Arbor. The rooms had felt clean and large, for her father had taken most of the furniture and pictures, and two of the oriental rugs, for his new household.

At first, she'd stuck to her Ph.D. work, completing her oral exams and writing a prospectus, but as the second summer came, her days had begun to feel like gorgeous bowls, each one a different shape, to be filled in ways she hadn't anticipated. Her stories had first come to her then, the ones for children, springing out of her typewriter in between pages about elegy in the modern novel. It had taken her years even to contemplate finding someone to publish them.

Rose went inside and listened to the quiet of the front hallway. She walked into the dining room and touched one of Sophie's paper constructions, a delicate tower made of paper, colored with crayons and scotch-taped together, with little windows cut out in different shapes. That second summer had brought her William too. For weeks he would amble past the house, a good-looking man with a slight dip to his walk, books and papers held loosely in his hands. She discovered that she came to know precisely when he would walk by: once in the early morning, and once in the late afternoon. He never seemed to come back the same way, although Rose had become aware that she looked for him, sometimes sitting in the dining room or on the porch with her research.

Rose climbed the stairs, and began to undress for her shower. She hung up William's bathrobe, and her nightgown, and bent over the white porcelain tub with the funny old claws. She turned on the shower and stepped into the tub, her belly huge and taut. She remembered how she had first met William. She'd been kneeling near the sidewalk in the early morning, plucking old flowers off the yellow marigolds when she should have been working, immersed in their pungent smell, when she heard someone walk by. A moment later she heard a shuffling sound, a clearing of a throat, and she looked up to see the slender man with the books. Pretty flowers, he'd said, looking enormously shy, and she had laughed. Thank you. Just marigolds, a humble flower. Very bright for humility, he had said, and she had looked at him more closely, seeing the scar on his right eyelid, the shape of his mouth.

Rose shampooed her hair. The funny thing was, she had not expected anything from this town. She had come back for the house, because she could not bear to think of it in other people's hands, and the garden too, and the little stretch of sidewalk where her mother had planted holly bushes. And now here was William L. Haas standing on the sidewalk, and she could tell by looking at him that he would become important to her. That very morning she walked with him to Luke's for breakfast, into which she had not stepped foot since she'd been on dates in high school. With sun streaming in, and fried eggs and toast in front of her, the whole restaurant had changed. The shops on Broadway too had looked suddenly real to her and full of life. After break-

31

fast, William had loped into the drugstore and then across to the appliance store, and she had followed him, amazed to realize she actually lived here again.

Drying her hair in front of the steamy mirror, Rose looked at the mess: Elizabeth's china animals paraded along the sill, dirty clothes lay in the corner, and someone had smeared toothpaste on the wall. I should clean, thought Rose, but she slipped on her old sundress and her thongs and walked down the stairs and out into the sunlight.

III. 200 Broadway

i.

At one o'clock the house at 200 Broadway dozed in the sun. Old wicker chairs sat on the porch, their arms embracing air. A yellowjacket hovered along the front walk, and two butterflies chased each other, skimming the daylilies in front of the porch and circling the columns. A tabby cat lay above the top step with her paws tucked under her, her eyes half-closed. An old woman walked by with a cane, her head bobbing.

To one side of the house a grape arbor arched. Old vines wove through the lattices. Along the fence and to the side of the porch ferns grew like fans in damp shade. Children's voices could be heard in the garden next door, as the click of croquet balls floated over the fence.

At the back of the garden, in the shade of a beech tree, a man sat in a faded deck chair reading. On the grass around him lay journals, pale pink and gray, and pads of yellow legal paper, but in his hands was a book. He had the air of someone looking for something, urged onward by an indefinable wish. His fingers held each page lightly, and the turning of a page mingled with the burr of grasshoppers and bees.

Upstairs, a woman lay dreaming, her face flushed. A large fan in a window whirred. As she moved onto her side her bare feet brushed a sheaf of papers, marked in type and red pen.

In her dream a baby sat, tight-fisted, holding a pen. Write this, it said, and Rose came close to listen, but the words sounded like trees. I can't hear you, said Rose, and the baby changed into a woman, its pink face clouded until it shaped itself into the face of her mother. Rose, said her mother. Rose.

"Rose?" A new voice, muffled and distant, came to her now on the borders of her dream. She looked at her mother

(Oh, stay, she thought), but already the dream trembled and tumbled Rose into the afternoon, her hair clinging to the nape of her neck. The warm air, a mesh of cotton, held her close on the bed.

"Rose?"

A sheet of paper floated to the floor.

Rose heard the screen door open on old hinges, and someone stepping into the hallway.

"Rose?" the voice called again, and in a rush Rose remembered Hallie. She sat up and rubbed her head.

"I'm up here!" she said, as if out of a cloud, and as she walked to the hallway she waved her hands in the air to push the cloud off.

"Hallie. I think I'm still dreaming." Rose held out her arms and walked down the stairs and into an embrace so tight that a laugh flew out with her breath. Her belly felt hard and awkward, as Hallie leaned into her. Over Hallie's shoulder Rose saw the cat stretching up on the screen door, its purr a question. She could feel Hallie's shoulder blades, and in a bright place of memory she saw Hallie sitting in a tree, her fingers stained dark purple, putting a berry in her mouth. Where had that been? She could not remember.

A second vision came to her, of Hallie's small back slender and curved as she bent to the floor, coloring. Once she had looked over Hallie's shoulder to see shades of blue: royal, and turquoise, and near purple. What is it about? Rose had asked. I can't see anything. It isn't about anything, it's just colors, Hallie had said.

Mitzi sat with an air of self-conscious patience on the porch, and Rose felt like a sailboat, the sail full-blown, as she walked to the door. The little cat rubbed gently against her calves and walked with her tail up into the dining room, where she jumped to a chair and began to lick her coat.

"She looks young," said Hallie, stroking Mitzi's head.

"She's seven months old." Rose watched Hallie's face grow soft as she squatted beside the chair, stroking Mitzi under the chin. "Oh, you're a beauty," she said. "Yes you are, and very intelligent too, I can tell."

The screen door banged and Sophie and Elizabeth came in, hot and arguing about the croquet game they had just been playing next door.

"Sophie cheated," said Elizabeth. "She moved her ball with her foot."

"I did not."

"I saw you, Sophie, and you kept taking extra turns."

Sophie began to cry and push against Elizabeth, and Rose sighed, embarrassed. Sophie threw herself onto Rose and clung, sobbing, as Elizabeth shuffled from one foot to another, looking miserable.

"Shush, shush," soothed Rose. "Look who's here. Do you remember I told you my old friend would be visiting today? She came a long way, and she wants to meet you."

Hallie stood up and smiled. She moved her hand toward Elizabeth, and then drew it halfway back, as if unsure what form of greeting to make. Rose felt pained for Hallie's shyness in the face of her children.

"I have pictures of both of you right in my studio, where I paint." Hallie spoke carefully, as if Elizabeth and Sophie were foreign dignitaries.

Sophie peered at Hallie through wet hands. "How did you get them?" she asked.

"Your mother sent them to me."

Sophie seemed to consider this, and then she said, "I can count to a hundred," and Elizabeth said, "Please don't," and Rose suggested that they find the popsicles in the freezer. Sophie followed Elizabeth into the kitchen with a sorrowful gait.

"I would have been glad to hear her count to a hundred." Hallie gave Rose a look at once full and uncertain.

Hallie had written to her after each miscarriage, quiet letters, how many now? Five, at least. Rose thought of her babies' duckling heads and the baby smell that had made her faint with joy. As if responding to her thoughts, the new one inside her gave a sudden kick, and she addressed it, and you too, I will have you too to hold in the early morning. You'll make your sucking noises and the world will condense to a milky circle, as the sky glimmers through the branches outside the window. In a wild rush Rose thought, I could give Hallie this child, and she pictured Hallie's joyous face, the baby a bundle in her arms, but in the next breath Rose thought, anything but this.

She looked out the window, across Broadway to the green space where Hallie's house had been. A picture came to her, absurd and magnificent, of an angel swinging down from those high trees, holding a bunch of marigolds. What Hallie longed for could come to her somehow, with real weight, to knock on her heart. The trees seemed to shake with gold, and Rose felt a lightness in the wish.

ii.

Hallie sat in a wicker chair on Rose's back porch, her sandalled feet in the sunlight. The garden seemed to wave to her, a proud and lovely wash of deep pinks and lavenders, and, in the shade, low white blooms. Close by the kitchen steps, pungent herbs grew in an oval bed. Sophie had picked some for Hallie, placing them carefully on her knee and offering their names as if Hallie were royalty, and the green sprays dukes and duchesses come to court: "Lavender." "Thyme." "Oregano." "Mint." "Lemon verbena." "Ah," Hallie said with each newcomer. "Thank you."

At the back of the garden a blue shadow stirred under the beech tree. It rose, and bent, and stood again, and as it came closer it showed the shape of a person. "Is that William?" asked Hallie, and in a moment William moved into the sunlight, his fair hair uncombed and an awkward gait making him seem to lope as he walked.

William said hello to Hallie, and stood by the porch steps holding his book, looking at his feet and then laughing as he made a joke. The sharpness of his eyes surprised her. She sensed the thread between William and Rose, sent out and caught, woven, and tossed back, a light tossing, grounded in the knowledge of how easily the other could catch, how willingly the other would draw in the thread to come closer.

"What have you been reading?" Hallie asked, tipping her head to see the book's title.

William looked at the book as if seeing it for the first time, and raised his eyebrows. "Oh. Well, actually, it's William James. Essays. I have a lot of philosophy books, but I don't usually read them. I just like to know they're there."

Hallie laughed. "But this one actually is getting read."

"I like William James."

"You do?"

William thought. "Yes. He could ask questions like 'What Is the Meaning of Life?'" He opened his arms wide, as if to embrace the question.

"So, what is the meaning of life?" Hallie folded her arms.

"Oh, well." William assumed a comical look, shrugging his shoulders. But he added, as he looked at the garden, "I think he's saying you can only live well if you make the choice to believe in something."

"I would like to live well," said Hallie. "But I don't know if it's that simple."

"I don't either." William gave a rueful laugh and touched a pebble with his toe.

I love you, thought Hallie, for reading a book by William James under the beech tree and contemplating a pebble by your shoe. She wished, fantastically, to hear him say how he loved her too. She imagined writing to Morey in New York: I'm sorry. I have found the man I adore. He reads American philosophy and lumbers out of blue shadows. He is a teacher, a writer of books, and his hair is fair, and we will live together for the rest of our days.

William turned from Hallie to look at Rose. Their wedding had been in this garden. On the day of the ceremony, the sky had offered a strange light show, now bright blue, now scudded with clouds and soon dark and heavy. A sudden shower during the party had sent all of them running into the kitchen, laughing, and Rose and William took off their shoes and opened more champagne. Rose's face had shone, but when Rose hugged her goodbye, she had heard Rose's breath catch, and she had looked at her to see her face wet. William had stood on the front porch in a cream-colored suit, and as Hallie had looked over her shoulder from the sidewalk, she'd seen William holding Rose close.

Hallie had thought Rose would become a college teacher, like William. She'd always had a luminous intelligence, and a love for all sorts of books. She'd received a special award at Michigan for her dissertation, and Hallie had urged her to look for a teaching position. But something had happened, once Rose met William. She seemed to slow down, to grow content. I don't know, she'd say to Hallie on the phone, I'm not sure I'm cut out for teaching. She'd mention some stories she'd been writing for children, but nothing had come of that yet, and now she was doing some editing and looking after her children. It puzzled Hallie, and it made her angry too, toward William. Handsome, shy William. You couldn't fault him, not really, but what had happened to Rose? She was so smart.

A breeze came up now, heavy and fragrant, as Hallie looked at the herbs in her lap.

"Another hot day," said William. "Can I get you anything, Hallie?"

"Sure."

"Rose?"

"Yes, something cold. There's lemonade in the fridge. Is that O.K., Hallie?"

Hallie nodded, and William jumped up the porch steps, two at a time. Soon Hallie could hear the little girls, their voices shrill, shouting at each other somewhere inside the house. Rose shook her head and sighed. Leaning her elbows on her knees, she turned to Hallie and looked as if she wished to say something. Hallie could hear William inside, opening the refrigerator and putting ice in glasses.

"So tell me," said Rose. "How's Brooklyn?"

"Brooklyn's good. Hot, now."

"And how's Morey?"

"Morey's pretty good. Very busy."

Rose cocked her head. "And how are you?"

"I'm good. Well, I'm O.K." She looked at Rose's beautiful face. Rose's hair was still thick, with silver strands, and her hazel eyes looked a deeper green today than Hallie had remembered.

Rose opened her mouth to say something, when William came out to the porch with tall glasses of lemonade. He handed them to Rose and Hallie, and sipped the third, sitting on the top step.

"So tell us about your painting," Rose said then.

Hallie shrugged. "I think I've dried up."

Rose looked at her incredulously. "Dried up! I'm sure you haven't."

"It can happen."

"Don't be ridiculous."

Hallie laughed. "I knew you'd say that, Rose. I count on you to set me straight."

"I've often thought," said Rose, "that a dry spell is important."

"You think so?"

"Yes. It helps you figure out what's missing, anyway."

"You mean, like rain?"

"Rain, and green."

Hallie contemplated this.

"I hope you're right."

Rose smiled. "I'm always right. Aren't I, William?"

"Absolutely." William scratched his head and smiled at Hallie.

Hallie suddenly noticed how tired he looked, the slight pouches under his eyes. "So you come to dry spells too?"

"Oh, yes. I'm a great believer in dry spells."

"Oh, stop," said Rose. "I'm going to pick both of you some mint for your lemonade." She pushed herself out of her chair slowly, and walked down the steps into the garden.

IV. Virginia

On Sunday morning Virginia Greaves lay with her eyes closed listening to Charles putter around the pool. And why should I open my eyes, when I know precisely what he will look like? With his old bathing suit and his brown back, his silver hair too long and curling on his neck and sweat glistening on his forehead and dripping into his eyes so that he has to stop and put down the long net and wipe his face with his shirt. I know you, Charles Greaves. I know how careful you are to skim the pool's blue surface and to catch all the flies and leaves and make the water clear, but what does it matter? You always focus on the wrong things. Look at your life, in this two-horse town. Who would ever expect to settle down here until the day they died? You are so dogged. Dogged, like a dog in stubbornness and self-centeredness. I have never seen such a man for giving the "yas-suh, yas maam," and then going ahead and doing whatever you goddamn well please. You don't fool me, not for a minute. It's that old Baptist upbringing, shine your shoes and put a dimple on your face, sing to Jesus. But what does it matter? What is it about?

Charles, as if hearing her thoughts, broke into a jaunty but elegant rendition of "Rock of Ages." "Shelter me, Let me hi-i-de myself in thee."

"Save it for church," shouted Virginia.

"What's that you say, dear?" Choir-boy manner, thought Virginia. You do it just to tease.

"Save it for church."

"Actually, I'm not going to church this morning. I thought I would have my own little service right here by God's own waters."

"Chlorinated," shouted Virginia. "God's chlorinated waters."

"Can't hear you, dear. You'll have to come outside if you want to have a conversation."

Bastard, thought Virginia, but she remembered how she had adored Charles in college, not only for his passionate nature but also for the stubborn morality that had made a date with him something heavy and delicious, always skirting the forbidden.

Hallie knocked lightly on the door and Virginia opened her eyes for a moment to see her daughter's face.

"Mom?"

Virginia gazed at Hallie. I should speak, she thought. My daughter.

"Yes, Hallie."

"I was just wondering, would you like to come with me for lunch somewhere?"

Virginia felt a stupor well up inside her, thickening her heart and slowing down her blood. Hallie's voice sounded distant, as if she were calling to Virginia through an invisible cotton mesh. "You have lunch, that would be nice, but you know I'm so tired, I think I just need to lie here."

Virginia closed her eyes and listened to the slap, slap of Charles's net on the water and to a neighbor's dog barking. A small drone of crickets started up, and she had a vision of crickets covering every inch of their property, pressing against the windows until they found a way in and clustered in piles on the carpet and on her bed. We could be in the Amazon, she thought, you could die here and nobody would know.

When she opened her eyes again Hallie was still there, sitting in the armchair.

She had been a gorgeous baby, with waving brown hair, a real charmer. And she had been so good, playing quietly in her crib, making little noises, each afternoon when Virginia slept. As she grew older, she would draw and read for hours, and when you spoke to her she would start, and when she looked at you over her drawing she would not recognize you at first, as if you were a stranger.

Hallie stirred in her chair, and paper rustled. Virginia opened her eyes to see Hallie holding a little package in white tissue paper.

"I brought you something."

"Oh. What is it?"

"It's not really a present, it's just photographs of some of my paintings. I wanted to get you a present, but I didn't have a chance, and I wasn't sure what you'd need."

Virginia took the photographs. She looked quickly at the pictures of white and gray, with little arrows and shadings, a few words too small to read. She felt at a loss. What were these about?

"You know I'm a complete idiot about art."

"No, you're not. They're just images, sort of abstract. You can think of them as landscapes seen from the air."

"I see. And the arrows are to show you which way to go."

"Yes, in a sense."

"Hm." Virginia looked at the last one and then folded the photographs up again in the paper. She held them out to Hallie.

"Oh, they're for you," said Hallie. "I have extras."

How did she get to be this way? thought Virginia, painting on canvases, pictures you could not understand. Virginia thought of her grim trips to museums as a child in Philadelphia. Her mother would dress Virginia up, with gloves and a hat, and drag her to look at old pictures and furniture. Once she had wandered into a room to see a naked woman in a big painting. Not that Mother would have allowed that, oh heavens no, flesh? Sex? She must have been a riot in bed. A cold woman. May she be in a heaven filled with nudes.

"Well." Hallie stood up. "I guess I'll go out by myself. You're sure you don't want to come?"

"You go ahead."

Virginia remembered how Hallie would come home from a date with bright eyes, her lips looking full, especially the summer when she'd go off with the one six years older, with long hair and a slippery look. He barely said hello, and Hallie acted as if it were all completely normal, Goodbye Mom tossed over her shoulder, her hair gleaming from the shower, her skin smelling like talcum powder. The thought of Hallie in a car with him, or with any of the others, had made Virginia shudder.

Virginia listened to Hallie's footsteps as she went down the stairs. Hallie said something to Charles and Charles responded, "Fine. Fine." A bit later Virginia could hear the car backing out. Hallie, she thought, come back, and then a huge splash seemed to make her bed tremble, as Charles dove into the pool and began to swim. She saw him in her inner eye, one arm arching and then the other, the stroke he had learned as a boy in Lake Michigan, where his family had gone two weeks out of every summer, deliberate, regular, water streaming down his face, and she thought of his body and his hands, and how seldom he had come into this bed for anything but sleep in the last ten years. It was not always so, she addressed him, you were hungry for me and could not wait until we got into bed, you would want me as soon as you walked in the door, and I was happy to have you. And when I was nursing the baby you would tremble for me to come back to you.

The bright sun came full into the room, above the curtains. A yearning shook Virginia for that baby, and for that man swimming.

V. Jesus

These roads are too small, Hallie thought, as she neared the top of a hill and slowed for a boy pumping a bicycle up the slope. A vision arose of a slow and magnificent crash, two cars meeting in the middle of Ohio on a road the size of a ladder. The sound would resemble heavenly cymbals, and the cars would rise in the air as in a dance and make slow arcs to the ground, where they would come apart into a thousand pieces of glinting metal and old tire. All of Ohio would listen, in amazement, and the people would talk for years of the mighty encounter. In the meantime, cabs would rush about New York, just missing each other, carrying people safely to their destinations, oblivious of this small, quiet world where cars could rise into the air and shatter.

This morning had been difficult. Each time Hallie had attempted to talk to her mother, the conversation had gone nowhere. You couldn't even call it a conversation. She'd offered her toast and jam, or a cup of coffee, but her mother had said I'm not hungry, I'll just wait a bit. And now she asked her about lunch, and she said she was too tired. A few times Hallie had sat near her mother's bed, bringing up subjects she thought her mother might like to talk about: her old friend May, books, the raspberry patch below the terraces, anything cheerful or at least neutral. But her mother seemed to have no heart even for these things. I never see May anymore, now that she's married to that idiot, she would say. I haven't read a good book in months. The raspberry patch has grown wild, as far as I know. Hallie had felt like shaking her, and in the next moment, saddened, she'd wondered whether it was her own presence that caused her mother to lose all interest in the world.

A mongrel dog sniffed at a mailbox to the side of the road, as the two mulberry trees near the pasture held court to the bees. She had come to these trees, a half-mile from her house, only with Rose. This had been their special place, once Hallie had moved. Hallie remembered a hot August day, dusty and brilliant, sitting in the branches of these trees with Rose. The berries had a gritty texture, and a sweetish bitter taste, but the glistening shapes of this dark fruit had made the trees seem to shimmer. Rose had had the idea to stain each other's chest with a mulberry thumbprint. Because we're really sisters, she had said solemnly. The juice is the tree's blood.

The first summer in the new house, Hallie had discovered raspberries on their property, and she had brought her mother down past the terraces to pick them. Her mother had held a bowl, and Hallie had added her berries to her mother's. Sometimes, walking back to the house, her mother had held her hand.

As she wound around curves in the road and began the steep descent into town, Hallie began to hear bells, their rich notes heavy. As a child, listening to those bells, Hallie would sit up straight in the car beside her father, dressed up and heading to church. Sunday School had smelled of chalk and her teacher's perfume, and Hallie had liked all the coloring and the songs.

Yes, Jesus loves me,
Yes, Jesus loves me,
Yes, Jesus loves me,
The Bible tells me so.

Driving slowly through the heart of town, Hallie found herself in front of the Baptist Church, a trickle of people walking in Sunday dress toward the front doors, where the minister greeted them in a long black robe. The church presided over Broadway in huge gray stone, and as Hallie stopped for the light she felt an urge to join that group of people in ties and pale dresses.

The light turned green and Hallie crossed the intersection to park half a block down, in front of the appliance store. She looked at an old couple walking arm in arm, and to their nods and "Nice morning" she dipped her head and smiled. Noticing the old woman's knobby Sunday shoes and her crimped hair, Hallie glanced at her own bare legs and sandals. Her legs looked pale and she wished suddenly to buy stockings at the drugstore, and to pull them on in a bathroom, but the heat of the day had begun.

The Episcopal church stood next to the Baptist church, its white columns and classical shape soothing still to Hallie. As a child, she had wished to be one of Rose's sisters, sitting in those crimson pews. She remembered one Sunday, when Rose had invited her to come with the Banfords to church, and she'd sat between Rose and her little sister Hannah, and through the whole service she'd studied Mr. Banford's handsome face. He was writing with a pencil on one of the programs, and when he looked up at one point he'd caught her staring at him. He had winked at her, and she'd felt a hot blush rise to her cheeks and her forehead. Just the night before, she'd sat with Rose at the top of the stairs at the Banfords' house, catching glimpses of the noisy partygoers below, the women in their cocktail dresses and the men in pale blue or white shirts. After dessert, the women had kicked off their shoes, and someone had pushed back the sofa and chairs in the living room for dancing. Hallie had gazed through the railings to see her mother, young and pretty in a black dress, scooped in front, and Mr. Banford pulling her by the hand to dance.

Hallie tripped on the curb and stubbed her toe, glancing quickly around to see whether anyone had noticed, but the mild-eyed elderly woman just behind her was making a careful study of her own shoes as they rose to the curb. Hallie flushed, and little needles of sweat broke under her arms and on her forehead. I'll go back to the car, she decided, but the thought of her mother lying on the bed made her hesitate. What could she do for her? The whole thing was impossible.

Walking into the vestibule of the Baptist church, a scent of lemon polish greeted her, mingled with other scents: old books, flowers, and something else, maybe the sweetness of grape juice and bread, and the sharp smell of coffee brewing downstairs in the welcoming area. Stained glass windows loomed on both sides of the church. When she was little, she had believed that Jesus sat high up, on top of one of the windows, and observed the whole congregation. Her teacher had said Jesus could look into your heart and know what was there, and this thought had both comforted and disturbed her.

Hallie found a seat toward the back. Around her in the large half-circle of pews people studied the service or gazed at the organist, who had begun to play a rich, deep-murmuring piece. An air of calm, almost of sleep, seemed to cover the whole community. How my mother would laugh, Hallie thought, to see me here, and immediately she felt self-conscious and foolish. Surely these people could see how out of place she was, her heart compact with a stubborn refusal to accept.

Her mother had accompanied Hallie to church only once, as far as Hallie could remember, and that had been for Hallie's baptism, a disappointing affair, and upsetting too, the way the minister pulled her back into the deep, cold water and held her there for a long moment. Coming up heavy and dripping from the water, and walking clumsily up the stairs of the baptismal font, her wet robe clinging to her and her white handkerchief a soggy ball, she'd felt something slipping inside her. She had thought the world would be different, once she emerged from the water. She had thought she'd be able to see clearly, maybe even see the divine in things, or see God in the clouds. And maybe her mother too would look happier, less distracted. But it had been just water, after all. Walking to the car in the spring evening, afterward, she had been quiet. So this is what's on the other side, Hallie had thought: wet, and cold, and the hard edges of real things, just as before, only worse, because I'm no longer looking forward to being changed.

Hallie's mother had gone to the Congregational church, as a child in Philadelphia, at least for Christmas and Easter, and maybe a scattering of Sundays each year. Hallie had asked her once why she never came to church anymore. Her mother had looked thoughtful. Well, I'm not a member of the Baptist church, she'd offered. But you could join it, couldn't you? Hallie had asked. I guess I don't think it's necessary, she'd said, and when Hallie had pressed her, she had added, Maybe I'm not sure I believe in all that. Hallie had felt shocked. How could her mother simply say she didn't believe? Do you believe in Jesus? she'd asked. A funny look had come into her mother's face then, and she'd said, Well, I'm not sure, Hallie. But lots of people do. Don't you think He's in church? Hallie had asked. Sometimes people say God is in your heart, her mother had said then, and Christ too. In my heart? Hallie had wondered at this, and conceived the idea of her heart as a little room, into which God and Christ could come. Maybe they would sit and talk, pass the time of day, or maybe they'd play checkers, as Hallie did sometimes with her mother's friend May. But isn't Jesus in church too? she had asked, and her mother had sighed and said, Maybe, but if there is a Christ, I'd rather think he was out there in the world doing something useful for once. Useful? Hallie had asked. Helping people, her mother had explained. Fixing things. Making things better.

A ripple of anticipation passed through the congregation, like the bend and rustle of a field as a breeze passes over it. Hallie looked up. The minister stood at the pulpit, holding its sides energetically. She had never seen him before. His face was aquiline and florid with a touch of heaviness about the jowls, his hair a shock of white. He brushed the church with a sharp gaze, and then his voice boomed out.

"The Lord be with you."

"And also with you."

"Amen."

The organ began a hymn. A flutter of pages filled the air, and with a slow and creaking movement the congregants arose to sing.

The music plunged to Hallie's bone. It was the words that did it, and the resounding determination of the quarter notes, their slow rise and fall circling back again and again with each verse. *O God, our help in ages past, Our hope*

54

for years to come, Our shelter from the stormy blast. Hallie sang with her eyes not even on the book, the hymn in her blood whether she wished for it to be there or not. The voices around her joined in wisps, like mist curling off a meadow.

Books closed with dull thuds. The congregants coughed and sat down, and Hallie wondered about the women around her. Had their insides been scraped too? Had they borne loss? the thick blood, metal on the inner flesh, where new life was supposed to have been? Surely they had not always felt as obedient to life's injuries as they looked now. That woman there, two rows ahead, her hair like a bird's nest and her shoulder-blades as thin as wings beneath her rayon print: an air of disappointment surrounded her like a cloud. Maybe she had a child or two, thought Hallie, and they disappointed her as they grew up, unhappy and rude, or maybe her efforts to conceive led to a whole sequence of fillings and emptyings, and her husband (Hallie measured the man sitting next to her, his hair thinning)—how had he responded? Had he quietly shut the door that was his wife's womb, and walked away? Did he see his babies' faces as he poured coffee at work, or started up the mower, or stared in the darkness of the bedroom at his wife's back?

Hallie thought about blood, how it had poured out of her, bright red, in banners and also in bundles of flesh, composed of blood vessels and clots. The last time, she had not been able to let the baby go—for it had felt like a baby, coming out of her with such fullness. She had not hesitated, but had scooped up the largest piece from the toilet bowl in the bathroom at that restaurant near Washington Square, and she had gazed at it for minutes, touching it, as if she could find a tiny body. But there was no body, and, cramping, she had wrapped the flesh in paper until she could see no more blood, and then she had put it in her purse. She had not told Morey right away. They were at the restaurant with Howard and Anna, and all through dinner, she had felt like a shell surrounding a precious secret, a matter of threads and fibers now, and blood like scented oil. As she drew her nightgown over her head that night she told him. He wept then, more than ever before, a sudden and fierce weeping, as he stood bent over at the sink, his hand covering his face

It wasn't easy to say goodbye to tiny bodies you couldn't even see. In your imagination, already they were babies, their skin glistening, their eyes barely opening, fists in mouths. But flesh could just dissolve. For Morey it was different, it must be, or how could he keep talking now about adopting? How could you adopt without pushing the others aside? For two years now, the subject had come up: babies from China, babies from Brazil, from Alabama. Morey urged her for a baby from anywhere, of any color, just a little person to hold to. But all Hallie could see, each time he spoke about it, was her own babies, as if they had almost been born.

"The heavens are telling the glory of God," said the minister. "And the firmament proclaims his handiwork," murmured Hallie, glancing at the service. "Day to day pours forth speech, and night to night declares knowledge." "There is no speech, nor are there words; their voice is not heard." In the early months of knowing Morey ("he has set a tent for the sun, which comes forth like a bridegroom leaving his chamber") she had felt touched by grace. His face had been open and his eyes alight with ideas and love—Come to the exhibition. Come to the restaurant. She saw him standing always in sunlight, his forearm sturdy as he held her hand to pull her out of the grave. Up, up, she walked, but had she reached the ground ever to stand next to him? Always she saw herself a foot or two away from the surface, Morey still pulling.

It must have been hard for Morey too. Across the table at Morey's mother's apartment, Hallie could see the traces of all she loved in him ("More to be desired are they than gold, . . sweeter also than honey"), but a sadness had moved into his face. It made his eyes turn down and pulled at his mouth. He was getting older ("Clear thou me from hidden faults").

Hallie looked up to see the choir rising. The organ crashed and dove, and the choir began to sing.

56

How to understand this marriage business? Could marriage become a wrestling match in the desert, with no angel, and no dawn, just two mortals pinned to each other, fighting to pluck out eyes, to injure throats? Sand and dirt the only witnesses. But, from across the table, Morey could smile, and the desert vanished. What had he joked about to his mother? "Hallie's not a shopper"—was that it? or "Hallie may become a New Yorker yet." Something silly, but he smiled, and Hallie thought, I love you for that smile. The landscape between them became lush again, and she hungered for his sweetness.

Mustard seed. That was what the minister was talking about. Jesus said the Kingdom of God is like a mustard seed. Hallie thought about Rose, for Rose's mother had been Mustard Seed in *A Midsummer Night's Dream* when she had been a girl in England, and Rose had asked her to tell them what a mustard seed looked like. Well, I was really a fairy, her mother had said, and I was quite little. Mustard seeds are, you know. Little.

Hallie tried to listen to the minister. His voice rose and fell, his arms waving in the air. "Jesus is like that mustard seed," he was saying. "We may think nothing of Him, we may toss Him across the field, and imagine such an insignificant thing has no place among our other crops, all our important activities each day. But, and this is the miracle, Jesus has the capacity, the divine capacity, given by His Father, to grow and spread within us." Hallie imagined herself as an overblown flowering tree, with the face of Jesus on the trunk, his arms the branches. "He is the Kingdom of God. In accepting His miraculous presence we embrace God's Kingdom on earth. You ask, how can this happen? And Jesus answers, if you open your heart to this smallest seed, God will do the rest. God will do the rest."

The minister turned off the light at the pulpit, and the organ began the last hymn. Protect me, thought Hallie, as the music rushed into her. I cannot bear this absurdity. But she stood, a congregant, and sang.

VI. Charles

Where the hell, thought Charles, Sunday at noon. Where the hell. He fumbled with the bills on the bookshelf in the living room, white and pale yellow rectangles with plastic windows. He had put his watch right here this morning, before he had cleaned the pool. It had gleamed, with the sun on it, right by those keys. How could it be gone? He looked higher on the bookshelves. A fine layer of dust covered the white wood. I keep losing things, he thought. Yesterday it was my glasses. And last week it was that note from the M.D. in Dayton, and I hadn't even had a chance to read it. I'm getting old. Each day I'll lose one more thing, until I'm sitting in a home, drooling and smiling my toothless smile at the nurses as they slap me another pill: Here, Charles. It's good for you. Just one more.

A vision of his mother came to him. She sat, her back straight, in her brown dress, at the breakfast table in his childhood house in Cincinnati. Her hair looped around her ears, held in place by little black bobby pins. Eat your breakfast, Charles, she said. Her eyes looked small behind her gold-rimmed glasses. But sometimes his father would wink at him or tousle his hair. At the lake his father would stand waist-deep in the water, teaching him to swim. You've got it now, Charlie, he would shout, and the pine trees waiting by the shore would look like tall candles, lit by the sun in celebration of his feat. At night Charles would listen to the lapping of the water and smell the pines and his father's pipe smoke curling into his bedroom from the tiny front porch. Even his mother had changed at the lake; once he had seen her dive from the rock, her plump arms arching over a flowery yellow cap. I'll beat you to the raft, his father had shouted, and she had raced him, in a spray of laughter and white water, until she reached the raft. She'd sat on the edge, pulling off the cap and drying her hair, as his father held onto the ladder. She had looked almost pretty.

I'll bet it's upstairs, Charles thought. I must have left it by the bed, and he felt heavy as he took the steps, feeling the carpet (new ten years ago) beneath his bare feet. In the bedroom, the light took him by surprise. Ginnie lay on the bed, as still as a statue in a Spanish church.

"Have you seen my watch?" he asked, and the statue moved slightly. Ginnie uncrossed her feet and crossed them the other way.

"Your watch. No, I have no idea where it is."

Charles wished to touch her feet, rub his thumb along the middle of the sole. The habit of holding off seemed like a heaviness inside him. His legs and hands felt large, and his heart seemed to beat weakly in his frame. He walked around the bed to sit on his own side. He looked at the bed-stand dully, wondering what was wrong. What had he been looking for? A pen and some coins lay on the stand, with a few receipts. Outside the window the little dogwood stood gracefully at the edge of the lawn. It was something to look at in the springtime, with its white blossoms, each stained red at the tip.

The dogwood was green now, fusing with all the greens of the woods edging the yard. And it had been deep green, dusky, the evening Ginnie had stood in a doorway, her hair uncombed, her face flushed, like a womanly tree. A face over her shoulder. You can have pictures of someone you keep in your heart, and sometimes that's the last time you see them like that. I knew right then, thought Charles, how much I had lost.

"Ginnie."

"Mm."

He lay looking at her mouth, the thin line it made.

Ginnie opened her eyes and stared at him. "What?"

"Are you all right?"

She seemed to muse on the question, to find humor in nuances too subtle for him to comprehend.

"If you mean, am I at death's door, I would say, no. If you mean, are you happy, is your life in order, I would also say no. How about you?"

Charles felt like crying. He had an urge to grasp her face in his hand and squeeze it, pushing her head back into the pillow.

Ginnie looked away. He pictured her lying on the bed at the old house, her face fierce and distorted. He had been a young doctor then, putting in long hours with child after child, sore throats and runny noses, stomachaches and fevers, just as it always was. Occasionally something terrible happened: the Taylor child dead at seventeen days, Angela Clifford with leukemia, the little Gates girl with the congenital heart defect. It was good, at first, to feel you were patching up the world, fixing whatever could be repaired. But the world keeps coming up with new rents in the garment. Charles saw himself in a fantastic picture, wearing his white coat and sitting on a big ladder with a huge sewing needle, sewing and sewing an immense robe, or curtain. Maybe Emerson was right, old man Emerson, in those essays Charles had read at college. How terrible to see behind the curtain, all decked out with blue sky and divine light.

Ginnie's hatred for him had seemed to come out of just such a blue sky. What had she shouted at him? that she could not live here for the rest of her life, she could not bear it. Hallie was standing by the bed wailing, her fairy hair rumpled, her face screwed into a tight ball. Charles had stood in the doorway. His wife and his child. All of it could shatter so easily. A sense of immense failure rushed over him, chilled his flesh in the middle of this hot morning.

Lord, I am unworthy. A picture of his father's library door rose before him. Behind the door, his father sat in an old leather chair, reading. He was always tired after his long days at the store. Life had been a disappointment to him, Charles thought. He had been an intelligent man. He could have prepared for the ministry, for he loved to discuss things, and he was a man of integrity. Money had been tight, though, and Charles's grandfather had urged him into the family business, a store of fine woolens. Charles could see Tilly in the kitchen washing the dishes, and his mother writing something at the kitchen table. Hush, Charles, she said. What had he been doing? Whistling, maybe, or laughing as he told Tilly about the dog he'd seen that afternoon, while she stood at the sink, her arms red from the washing, and each plate came out of the second sink clear and streaming. Tilly liked dogs. She had had a dog— Muffy? or Suds? something Irish, for Tilly had been Irish (a mackerel-snapper, his father said) and went to the Catholic church. Maybe they were allowed to make more noise in her house, and in her church too, because Tilly never minded noise. She laughed with a short, sharp laugh when he would tell her about the boys after school, running in the alleys behind the houses.

Charles rubbed his head and his eyes. Tilly was long dead, in brown earth. She had given him a present when he had won his scholarship to Yale, a bookmark with angels on it, trumpeting. It had looked a bit ridiculous to him, the flimsy angels and their glittery trumpets no match for the trouble life held, but he loved Tilly, and thanked her for it. She had given him two dollars too, a lot of money in those days. He had tried to give it back to her, but she wouldn't take it. "It's for you to have a bit of fun now and again, to buy a malted or go to the pictures. I'm sure you can find places to spend it, Charlie."

Ginnie had begun to breathe more deeply, and Charles could tell by the way her cheek softened that she was asleep. A memory came to him, of walking into the old house on Broadway in the middle of the afternoon one day, and seeing Hallie small in her crib, sitting up and talking to herself. Such a sweet kid, waiting for Ginnie to wake up. He had come into her room, and her wisps of hair had smelt like something delicious, apricots or vanilla. Lifting her out of her crib, he had felt astonished by her beauty.

Charles closed his eyes and saw orange and yellow, queasy colors. Hallie had seemed to hold all that was good in the world, all that was healthy, fine, straight, and lucid. Washing her back as she had sat in the bath, listening to her singing, seeing her delicate shoulders, her face finely cut and infinitely soft, her legs held straight out, her toes pink in the warm water, he had been astonished to have something like this in his life, like a Christmas present always at the moment of the first unwrapping, shiny and new. Her preciousness had frightened him.

Charles felt his eyes sting and rubbed them: crying, was he? Here she was, like a foreigner, with her elegant haircut and the way she had of tilting her head and looking at him as if she could not understand one thing he said. Charles longed for her smallness again, her pink toes and her childish grace.

VII. Blue

On Monday morning, in the blue space before dawn, Hallie woke sharply. The room looked odd. Where was the light? Always the light from the street made the white material over the windows glow, so that she could see Morey sleeping. The air was warm and humid, and strangely quiet. The sheets felt soft, twisted damply, clinging to her legs, and the pillow was wet where her face had been. She saw two squares of blue, windows, but how could windows change shape while she slept? She drew herself up on her elbows. Of course. She had forgotten where she was. A thin light from the hall shone under her door, and outside the blue windows was Ohio.

When she woke again the walls in the room had grown brighter, turning to a lighter blue tinged with dusky yellow. The ordinariness of objects was beginning to emerge again: the angles of the desk and chair, her bag on the floor next to her sandals. I could paint this, she thought. Blue on darker blue, with fine lines of white, and luminous squares maybe of another color. She felt suddenly hopeful, picturing herself in her studio, stretching a new canvas. The traffic would sound faint rumbling in the street below, and above the building across the street she would see the sky, an airplane floating past in a silver shimmer. Maybe this one could work. I'll have to remember it.

The house was still. On a road far away a car rumbled. A mile from here cows were being milked and pigs fed. But the circle of trees around the house seemed to hold their breath and loom, the half-light sticking in their leaves. She untwisted the sheets and stood up. Brushing her hair, she studied the lines around her eyes and above her mouth; her face in the mirror looked pinched and swollen.

She remembered about her mother, how she'd stayed in bed all of Sunday, and how as evening came she lay in the darkening room until Hallie turned on the lamp by her bed. That's all right, her mother had said. You can turn it off, I don't need it on. Don't you want to sit up and read or something? Hallie had asked. But her mother had just shaken her head, and Hallie had turned off the lamp again. She'd hesitated by the door, wondering if she should try again to talk to her, but something about her mother lying there in the growing dusk had made Hallie uneasy, and she had quietly left the room.

I'll make a cup of tea, she thought now, putting on her robe. Downstairs the air seemed lighter. The trees outside had begun to take on color. The newspaper lay on the couch where her father had been reading before bed, and his glasses lay on the newspaper. Last night, as she had sat in a chair reading the paper, her father had said, Can I fix you a drink, Hal. No thanks, she had said, and she'd put on some hot water to have with lemon, for her throat had begun to feel raw. Her father had poured something in his glass and sat down to read another section of the paper, and as Hallie had waited for the water to heat up in the kitchen she had gazed at the blue counters and the dish drainer, a washrag hung over one side.

As she had sipped her lemon water, her father had put down the paper, his glasses tipped on the end of his nose. He looked at her with a soft expression, as if she puzzled him and he wished to understand. Are you all right? he had asked, and she had said, Yes, I'm fine, only a little tired, I think I'll go up soon, and he had continued to look at her with a kind of compunction. I'm afraid it wasn't much of a dinner, he said. It was fine, said Hallie. Would you like something more? No, really, thanks. I'm afraid this isn't much fun for you, he added after a moment. I 'm having plenty of fun, she said, and she had made an effort to smile.

Looking out the kitchen window now onto the terrace, Hallie envisioned, in one sweep, a new sequence of paintings, composed of windows at different angles to each other, and of various shapes and sizes. Squares, mostly, but of surprising beauty. Some could be haunting, dusky and shimmering, and some would shine in the height of day, but almost never would you see inside, except for the half-moon of a face or the line of a hand. Could these work? Hallie wondered. So often an idea came to nothing.

Someone made a sound upstairs. Hallie heard rushing

water, and then footsteps coming slowly down. Her father appeared in the doorway, with his hair rumpled and his pajamas etching a pale design.

"I thought I heard someone down here."

"I was just about to make some tea."

"You couldn't sleep?"

Hallie shrugged. "I'm fine. Do you always get up this early?"

"Most of the time. Your mother says I have no gift for sleeping."

Hallie smiled and looked at her bare feet. Her father's worn pajamas made her feel close to him, but awkward too. She thought suddenly of how, years ago, in Providence, a man in her neighborhood used to make his breakfast in the nude. She had walked past his house each morning, smelling coffee and sometimes bacon, and trying hard not to peer through the long, open front windows into the back of his house, where he stood at his stove with his middle-aged belly and flat rump.

Her father opened a couple of drawers and looked inside. "Have you seen my watch, Hal?"

"Maybe you left it outside."

Hallie looked out the window. On the terrace, a red bird alighted for a moment and quickly flew into the dogwood. She remembered how the dogwood's white petals had made a small canopy over her. While it was in bloom, she used to sit on the lawn under it, with her drawing paper and her crayons, feeling that somehow its lightness and grace would spill onto her pictures.

"Dad."

"Hm?"

"Do you think Mom is—what do you think's going on?"

Her father looked uncomfortable. He leaned against the counter. "I'm not sure."

"She says she gets up all the time."

"I know. She tells me that too."

"Well? Maybe she gets up when you're not here?" Hallie hesitated. "She says you're not here all that much."

"I'm here plenty. You know Matt has pretty much taken over my practice now. I'm just about retired."

"Yes, but you're busy with other things too?"

"Well, I go downtown sometimes. I have to shop, and do errands."

"I know. I'm not saying you should be here more. I just can't figure out what's going on."

Her father rubbed his temple. "I can't either."

"How long did you say she's been like this, so tired, not doing anything?"

Her father looked embarrassed, as if he felt at fault for something. "Well, it's gotten worse. She used to come outside, get the mail, look at the garden for a minute. And she used to have friends over still, but now that Lilian's gone . . . and of course you know Cheney died too, last summer."

Hallie pictured Lilian and Cheney, two of her mother's oldest friends, sitting in their straw hats by the pool when Hallie was young. Lilian would hold long, thin cigarettes in her bony fingers with the red nail polish, and Hallie used to gaze in fascination at the way the smoke would sometimes curl back up into her nostrils. Lilian always wore sunglasses and clothes that looked expensive. Cheney smoked too. When Hallie would come onto the terrace, Cheney would say, in her gravelly voice, Here's my girl! the one who's going to make the boys go wild. Hallie's mother had seemed by comparison awkward, almost doe-like. She had laughed at all their jokes, but Hallie hadn't been sure how she'd felt inside.

"What about May?" May had been Hallie's favorite. She loved books, and she only drank lemonade in the afternoon, and once she gave Hallie a new notebook of creamy white paper.

"May's in Florida most of the year now. She married again, you know, Frank. And the last time she came back, your mother told her she didn't feel well enough to see her."

"She didn't feel well enough? So has she seen a doctor? Could it be something?"

"I've taken her to the doctor. He says she's fine. He ordered all kinds of tests. I think she's . . . low. In spirits."

Hallie sighed. Her father and she had agreed somehow on this word, low, as the most descriptive one, ever since she was little. You and I are eating at Luke's tonight, he'd say. Your mother's feeling a bit low. Or, Sorry, Hallie, you can't have Rose over right now, your mother's low today. And low seemed accurate but confusing, for her mother lay horizontal on the big bed. Even though the bed was high, she was low. Hallie knew what he meant, though, and she knew how to walk on tiptoe in the hallway past her mother's bedroom, and she knew how to make her own breakfast, putting cereal into a bowl and pouring the milk slowly so it wouldn't spill.

"Could she see a psychiatrist?" She said this hesitantly, knowing how her mother detested the idea of talking to someone about her feelings. Hallie had suggested this on one of her visits just before her marriage to Morey. But her mother had snapped at her, I'm not paying money to some shrink in the middle of Ohio to tell me what's the matter with me.

"I've suggested that. She's not interested."

Hallie held her elbows, and her father sat down heavily at the table.

"Would you like a cup of coffee?" she asked.

"I can make one, Hal. How about you?"

"O.K."

He stood up and moved about the kitchen, as if glad to have an immediate purpose, pouring water into the pot and finding two mugs.

"Any news for you?" he asked, as he measured the instant coffee. "I mean, for you and Morey?"

Hallie felt like a nocturnal creature surprised by a flashlight. She had almost never mentioned her miscarriages to her mother and father. She had told them only about the first one, and after that she'd ignored the subject, saying only, No, nothing's happened yet. She'd written to them about the last one, though, and her father had written back, saying they were sorry, and they wished things could work out better.

Hallie shook her head. "I think we've given up."

Her father looked at her with a pained expression. "That's too bad."

Hallie's eyes stung.

"Your mother and I —" he began, but then he paused, and opened a drawer, pulling out two spoons. "Do you like milk? I forget."

"Yes, thanks." Her father opened the refrigerator and took out a carton of milk.

"You said, 'your mother and I —'?"

Her father looked confused for a moment.

"Well. Your mother will be sad to hear it."

"I really don't want to mention any of that to her. She seems sad enough already."

"Well, she's —. I know it's hard, sometimes, to get over such things."

Hallie looked at the milk carton. The water steamed, and her father poured it into the mugs. Hallie stirred milk into her coffee.

"I think I'll just walk outside for a moment."

"Good idea, Hal. I'm just going to water a few plants. Did you see the solarium? I've made it into a kind of green-house."

She looked at him quickly and smiled, shaking her head, her eyes wet.

"I'll come see it later."

Holding her coffee, she opened the door to the terrace and stepped out. The slate patio felt damp and smooth to her bare feet, and the sky above the trees looked clear and silver-blue. A yellow light touched the wild cherries, and a breath of air rustled the thick leaves. She walked down the steps to the pool and dipped her toes in the water, sending small ripples in fans to the other side.

Hallie turned to look up at the house, waiting in the morning hush. She caught a glimpse of her father, as he walked into the solarium and bent over to do something. Slowly she walked along the side of the pool, stepping over the wild cherries scattered at the edge.

VIII. Creek

i.

"This was where I saw the angel," said Rose.

Hallie smiled quizzically. "The angel?"

The creek glinted. It spread out wide in this part (as if to give itself time to think, thought Rose), and the rushing current met this deeper pool with little frothing exclamation points of surprise. Rose and Hallie sat on a blanket in a space clear of brambles. The light tendrils of a willow made a tent around them, and when a breeze came up the willow waved. It was Monday afternoon. The sun was hot, but as it achieved the top of the sky the air assumed a dry clarity so unusual in an Ohio July that the day seemed cut out of time.

The girls were at day camp this week, giving Rose a chance to catch up with everything, and to see Hallie too. This morning, as Rose had helped Sophie and Elizabeth make their lunches for Bushy Hill and find hats and sunscreen, she had remembered that Hallie would be leaving tomorrow—hadn't she said Tuesday? She may not see Hallie for another seven years (and this one will be long-legged then, a boy or a girl, which will it be?—Do you want an apple, Sophie?), and the thought had made her panic for a moment. People could just go out of your life. You might think long days shone ahead of you, when you could ask questions of each other, hands magically touching bone, able to plunge past skin. But look what can happen. I feel close to Hallie, but I barely know her husband, and how can I know what it's like to wake up in her apartment in Brooklyn and to see the cut of shadows at noon on a particular corner she comes to each day?

In the midst of this questioning, the baby had rolled heavily, and she had felt stunned by the thought of how new this person inside her was, and with what confidence she had created it with William. Having a baby seems so simple, in one sense. But sometimes (Stand still, Elizabeth, she had said as she brushed her daughter's hair, a barrette in her mouth) the momentousness of it comes to tap you on the shoulder. The labor and birth are one thing (Rose remembered the terror she had felt, with Elizabeth, the long hours and the unfamiliar faces, and the final shock of the forceps). But then there is daily living, and how can you be responsible for the ten thousand things that can happen out of the blue? The heart with only two chambers, the collapse of the lungs in a baby born too soon? Or if the baby is healthy at birth, safe in your arms, how can you foresee the rush across the street, the burn on the toaster, the face in the water, the cruelty of people who happen to notice your child and decide on something brutal? (You need socks, she had told Sophie firmly.)

"Well, she didn't look like an angel," Rose said now, "but I know she was one."

"What did she look like?"

"She looked like an old woman, with beat-up shoes—I think they were sneakers—and wispy hair."

"Ah. Your regular bag lady kind of angel."

"Yes."

"Where was she?" Hallie urged her body forward to look at the creek more closely.

"She suddenly appeared on a rock right next to me."

"Where were you?"

Rose hesitated. She had only told this to William. She caught an alarmed look on Hallie's face.

"I was sitting in the creek."

"In the creek? Rose, how could you?" Hallie held her elbows. "What about snakes? And mud? Isn't it very muddy and slippery on the bottom? You can't see your hand."

"I know, but somehow I couldn't worry about snakes that day."

"When was it?"

"It was a few days after my mother died."

At the edge of the water a dragonfly hovered, impossibly blue. It darted in quick lines to the blanket, to the mud, to a stone in the water, and at each new spot it shone.

Her father's voice on the phone had sounded distraught and hoarse, as if he had a cold. How could she die without me? she had thought then, and the question had set up a permanent residence inside her as she had driven from Oberlin along the highway, past lush fields and sleeping towns. A white space, a blankness, had opened up just under her skin, and she had had a vision of each barn, each cornered roof, as paper-thin, like the first ice.

Her mother's face had looked like plastic, strangely taut and yellowish. The crimson plush of the coffin, the ornate pillars of the funeral home parlor, what had her mother to do with all that? In the next moment she had appeared to Rose, alive after all though fine as air, hovering to the side of the dim front room of the funeral parlor. She had leaned on a pillar, her arms crossed and her hair in a helter-skelter bun, as if she had just been gardening. This is silly, she had seemed to say, shaking her head slightly, her eyes kind. Death isn't this, not at all (she waved her hand toward the coffin). Isn't it? Rose had asked her quietly, Look. The hard body, the face a mask. Oh, Rose, her mother had said.

"So tell me about the angel." Hallie traced the diamond pattern in the blanket.

"Well, she appeared all of a sudden, perched on the rock."

"She had walked through the water?"

"I know you'll think I'm crazy, Hallie, but she just appeared. She assumed form. Her feet weren't wet."

"Maybe she flew?"

"Well, she didn't have wings. She looked more like— well, like somebody's mother."

"But not yours."

"Oh no. Except that her hair reminded me of my mother's. It was fine hair, and slipping out of a bun. She had bobby pins sticking every which way."

Hallie laughed. "Oh, Rose, is this true?"

"Yes, it's true, absolutely. You don't believe me, do you?"

"I do believe you. Of all the people I have ever known, you are the one an angel would appear to."

"You've never seen one yourself?"

Hallie gazed at the edge of the water, her eyes narrowing. "Only you, Rose."

"Oh, I'm not an angel."

"How do you know?"

"Believe me, I know."

Hallie laughed. "So tell me more."

Rose thought. "She looked at me very kindly. She had brown eyes. And she asked me what I was doing."

"And you said, I'm sitting in the creek."

"Actually, I said, I am about to drown myself."

"Oh, Rose. Tell me that's not true."

"I thought it was true. I was so sad, and nothing seemed right. I can't tell you how my mother, dying like that, pulled all substance out of the world. I thought it wouldn't take much effort to die, and be out of the world."

Hallie looked contemplative. "And the angel?"

"She said, Hard to drown yourself in that little bitty creek."

"An angel with a sense of humor."

"Yes. And I said, I think I can manage it."

Rose paused. The angel had just shaken her head, and a breeze had come up, rippling the water and making the little trees wave their leaves.

"What happened then?"

"I looked into the water and saw minnows and tadpoles, and a large catfish hovering near the angel's rock. When I looked up, she was gone. But the strange thing is, I suddenly felt wet. I hadn't had any feeling at all, as if I'd been a paper doll, a joke, and now I felt heavy again, and wet. And muddy. And I could feel the little stones under my legs. And when I stood up, my dress was wet and covered with silt."

"You didn't try to drown yourself?"

Rose eased onto her back and shaded her eyes.

"I went home."

She had searched the house for clues to her mother, objects that could hold her mother in them: nail scissors, letters, a hairbrush, a hat. She would look up from her contemplation of an open drawer and see Catherine, pained and oddly eager, gaze into the drawer too, and suddenly she would wish to close the drawer, to say She is my mother, as if to shut Catherine out. As children, she and Catherine had made a game of this possessiveness: my mother, my mother, each would say, sitting on their mother's lap, kissing her, wrapping arms around her, pushing the other off. I love each of you completely, her mother would say, now let me up, but they would shriek with laughter, pinning her to the chair. My mother.

The sun was high, glancing through the willow tree in splashes. Hallie leaned on her elbow.

"Did you ever see the angel again?"

"Not that I know of. But—now don't laugh, Hallie—I sometimes used to see my mother."

"Why would I laugh at that? I only wish I could see her."

Rose looked at Hallie, her head ringed with long, cool willow fronds. As a child, Hallie had been like a third sister. If Rose's mother had been making dinner, one of the children in Rose's family would pull on her arm or yank her blouse or stand right in front of her, arms around her waist, the better to gain her attention. What, what, Rosie? she would say with impatience, a spoon in the air or the cat's bowl half-filled. Hallie would stand near the kitchen table, one knee on a chair, watching with a look of—hunger, was it? Avidity, certainly, for all of Hallie's unspoken wishes seemed to be carried through her eyes. And when her mother had included Hallie with Rose's sisters, in one harried gesture, as she said Set the table now, or All of you be off, let a body have some peace, Hallie had looked surprised and happy.

"She isn't always easy to see. I feel as if she's just behind me, looking over my shoulder, or maybe in the next room, behind the door, but when I turn around or look into the room I can't see her at all. If I'm lucky, she'll sit in a chair and have a conversation for a minute or two. But you know what's strange? I haven't been able to see her like that for months now, I don't know why. And I have this feeling that she's vanishing, and that one day I won't even feel her standing at my elbow."

"I'm sure she won't vanish completely."

"I'm not sure. I almost feel her saying, `I know you'll be all right now. I can leave now,' as if she's been staying just to be certain."

The baby rolled inside Rose. Maybe life held this out to her: the knowledge of absence, of air where something rich had been. Into this air her baby would come, glistening and distraught, its lungs opening as if cut with ice.

Rose gazed at the creek. How could it be that her mother and her father, the two people she had loved the most, had left this earth?

Rose thought of the parties her parents had held years and years ago, when she was little. Her father's voice would cannon above the others, from the garden, as he told raw stories in almost a parody of his own Yorkshire accent. She always knew how he would look, for often she and Hallie would tiptoe into one of the back bedrooms to peer out the window and catch a glimpse of him, in an open shirt and with his black hair uncombed, holding up a glass in one hand and a cigarette in another as he gesticulated, his face lit up by the porch light.

Often the figure next to him would be a woman. Rose could picture a hand on his forearm, lingering, or a woman's smooth head leaning close to his. Sometimes he would be with Hallie's mother, and their voices would fall to a murmur as Mrs. Greaves's hand would flick a cigarette ash into the damp gloom of the garden. Once Rose had seen him touch Mrs. Greaves's shoulder, caressing the strap of her dress. Had Hallie seen that too? She could not remember.

Rose pictured how her mother had looked at those parties, her hair brushed and shining, sometimes let down so that it floated on her shoulders. She would bring drinks to people, and plates of crackers, and she would sit on the arm of the sofa talking. Sometimes she would let Hallie and Rose pass plates of olives and little cheese biscuits. But she did not have her shoulder caressed by someone, thought Rose, her old anger at her father rising. By Sunday morning, he would look sober again, although paler than usual, and the cigarette flicking ashes into the garden, or the head on a shoulder, seemed to Rose like dreams. But once she and Hallie had woken in the middle of the night to hear something shattering, and her mother shouting, You bastard, you bloody bloody bastard. They had gone to the top of the stairs to listen, but all they could hear was her father's rumbling voice and her mother's sobs. How could he make her mother cry so? Rose had thought, I will never forgive him, never, but at breakfast he had smiled at her and Hallie, a gentle smile, as he helped Hallie tap her egg open, and poured cocoa for Rose. The milk had made the powdered chocolate swirl and she had felt her heart quicken.

"How about some lunch?" said Rose, opening her bag and peering inside.

ii.

Hallie gazed at Rose asleep under the willow. Rose lay with her legs curled up, her red hair scattered over her arm, bent to pillow her head.

How's your mother? Rose had asked, and Hallie had attempted to tell her. It was hard, though, talking to Rose about this. Hallie had often found it hard. Where's your mother? Rose would say, when they were children, and sometimes Hallie had made up something—Oh, she's out shopping, or She's seeing a friend—rather than tell Rose, She's in her room, asleep. Asleep?! she knew Rose would say. Sometimes Rose would urge Hallie to ask her mother a question, like, Can we go down to Mallow's and get a Coke? or, Can we go rollerskating? But usually Hallie would shrug and wiggle out of it. She couldn't bear the thought of opening her mother's door.

Is she all right? Rose had asked just now, and Hallie had said, Well, not really. What is it? Rose asked. She's just very low, Hallie had said. Is she ill? I don't think so. Rose had stared at her, and Hallie had wished to hide from her look. She's just very low, Hallie had said again, and Rose had nodded.

It was strange, the story Rose had just told her, about the angel. Hallie tried to piece together her memories of that spring. Hallie had flown back to Ohio from college in the middle of exams, as soon as she'd heard of Mrs. Banford's death. In the old graveyard on the hill, a few blocks from Rose's house, she had stood near the rectangular opening in the earth as the priest in the white surplice had spoken. Rose had looked odd, her hair only half-brushed, her eyes held to the coffin. This had been Hallie's first funeral, one of the only ones she had ever been to, really, except for Morey's father's funeral, and that had been completely different, partly because she had only met him a few times and partly because the coffin in the ground had formed only one moment in a week of family mourning, when each evening

Morey's cousins and aunts and uncles had come over, with old friends of his mother and father, to sit shiva. People had brought plates of food over each day, and after the service each night people had pushed the chairs back and poured out glasses and eaten sweet pastries and fruit. Morey had cried with Hallie, but in his mother's apartment he had been talkative and friendly, opening the door for guests and welcoming everyone. Hallie had never thought death could be accompanied by such festivity.

At Rose's house, friends had come by after the funeral, but a sensation of shock had prevailed. People had looked baffled, and Rose had become terribly quiet. Thank you for coming, she had said in the hallway by the stairs. Of course I had to come, Hallie had said, and Rose had hugged her hard.

In the car driving home, Hallie's mother had begun talking of other things, how terrible Ian Banford had looked, and how she had heard that Rose had a new boyfriend. You are merciless, Hallie had thought. All she could think of was Mrs. Banford lying in the coffin in the middle of Ohio, an ocean away from her original home, six feet of dirt over her, and Rose looking utterly bewildered. Hallie had barely been able to talk to her mother then, and the next morning she had flown back to school.

Hallie contemplated the fullness of Rose's lips and her upper arm, freckled and round. She felt the urge to curl closer to Rose, tucking her head into the place just beneath Rose's shoulder. How calm it must be for the baby, she thought, with Rose's blood rushing and soughing like trees in a high wind, or like water over stones. All morning Hallie had been aware of the life inside Rose, with its round head and its little buttocks, sucking its fingers and listening.

Hallie thought about how Rose's body was like a landscape she could see only from a distance now, one that she had known once and could not find again, certainly not in the same form, for she had changed. Rose's body had been the first one open to her, the first one she'd come to know, and maybe the only one in which she'd ever made a home.

To curl up together, to see how your bodies fit, to study each inch because each inch holds itself out to be touched and understood: scabs and warts, the birthmark between the big toe and the second, the dimples in the back, the curving space between the legs with its intricate whorls, its musty smells and whitish stickiness, the tiny round nub rising, and the fine hairs at the back of the neck, the wings of shoulder blades, the small moon of the belly, the tenderness of nipples.

If she could know Morey's body as she had known Rose's. If she could feel a right to his toes, the slenderness of his ankles, the tightness of his calf muscles. When she had first known him, she had marvelled at the hollow in the small of his back, the smooth skin of his belly, the thick curly hair of his groin. For a month at least, in the old apartment in Providence morning and afternoon and night, she had felt unafraid of his beauty; she had seen him as beautiful. What had changed? How had he come to seem opaque to her, indecipherable?

Her eyes stinging, Hallie rummaged through her straw bag to find her sketchbook and the tin of colored pencils. She hadn't sketched in weeks. Opening it up, she glanced at the last attempt she'd made, a sketch of the gray building across the street from her studio. She'd been thinking about going back to representation, but each sketch she'd made soon seemed dull to her, too flat somehow. She couldn't find the heart of it. And anyway, she'd almost forgotten how to draw.

Contemplating Rose, she began to make light motions, a design. She envisioned this one as pure color and shape. Around the edges would be swatches of crimson, maybe— and inside a burning blue, no, yellow, how about yellow? with half-curves, maybe in red. How to find colors to hold Rose? This morning's blues felt distant now, too cool for the heat Hallie felt on her legs and in her fingertips. As she worked, a sudden gaiety rushed over her, as if in choosing these colors she herself became bright, a sunny thing.

Rose sighed in her sleep and rolled her shoulders onto

the blanket, her arm above her head. Rose's cheek was wet where it had rested on her arm.

Hallie's mother would be sleeping too. Hallie turned to a new page of the sketchbook and rubbed it with her finger. A picture came to her, of her mother in bed in the old house on Broadway. Her mother's shape lay curved and muffled under blankets and pillows. One of the rules of the household, etched into Hallie's marrow, had been to allow her mother to sleep each afternoon. A second picture followed, dream-like: an arm swinging out from the pillow and the quilts, an angry face, a sharp slap to Hallie's back, and a voice saying Don't you ever wake me up again Don't you ever wake me up again.

She looked at the white page. Around it she saw the diamond patterns of the blanket, and her red skirt. Her toes were bare, and now she stretched one foot out past the blanket to rest on a tuft of rough grass. A little pathway made a brown line from the center of their blanket to the creek, through taller grass, and she could see a muddy flat by the water, and the gleaming surface of the creek, rolling slightly where it parted around a stone.

Rose woke up.

"Any angels?" she asked.

Hallie laughed and shook her head.

"I had such an odd dream." Rose combed her hand through her tangled hair.

"Did you?" Hallie looked at the blank page, and then gently closed her notebook.

"Yes. You were in it, only you were a child, and you kept trying to tell me something, but we were in a boat and the boat was tipping, and I had to be very careful to hold it balanced. I was afraid you'd fall out. I'd look at you, and you'd begin to say something, but then the wind would come up again and I couldn't hear you, and the boat would tip in another direction."

Rose rolled to her side. She looked at Hallie. Hallie looked away, reaching to pluck a grass blade and draw it through her fingers. She could feel the boat tipping, and she could picture Rose, big as life, on the boat, keeping it balanced.

"Should we head home?" asked Rose. She looked so healthy and right. Hallie stood up, smoothing her shirt. Rose held out her hand, and Hallie pulled her slowly up. Hallie put her notebook in her bag, and then she and Rose shook the blanket and drew its four corners together, once and twice and a third time. Rose handed the blanket to Hallie.

"Ready?" Rose's smile seemed full of the willow tree and the sun, the glinting water and the catfish near stones.

IX. Swimming

Monday afternoon. Virginia dozed. Her body felt light, buoyant, as if she lay on top of water, or tumbled slowly about in a watery world among long stems of lily pads and cloudy balls of frogs' eggs. She opened her eyes underwater, to see the brown bottom of a rowboat far above her. People in the boat cast shadows, and little silver hooks slipped quietly into the water. Fish swam in slow circles, shining pale iridescent. She was looking for something, a little fish hidden in the weeds.

"Ginnie?"

Fish swam, pale iridescent.

"Ginnie?"

The sound came muffled as Virginia swam in slow circles. Was it a fisherman peering into the water who had spied her? So pleasant here, the water at mid-day. I can float into the weeds and the fisherman will not see me.

A touch on her shoulder brought her almost to the surface. Charles sat on the bed, looking anxious.

"I've been calling your name for ten minutes. Are you all right?"

To sink down again is so pleasant. Leave Charles in the boat, such a worried fisherman, he will never catch a fish. And over there, a glint of a fish tail waving at her.

"Ginnie." The touch became rougher as he pulled her arm toward him. "How many sleeping pills did you take?"

Pills were little fish swimming slowly. Virginia swam with them, her arms young and slender, her hair a thick mass tangled in fish-weed, fish-eggs. She opened her mouth in little circles, her gills flapping open and shut.

"I'm going to call someone if you don't answer me. This bottle's almost empty."

Caw, caw, to the side of the lake the heavy crows do a silly two-step.

"Caw, caw," said Virginia.

"Can I get you something to eat."

Crows bob their heads up and down, one-two, one-two, pecking out entrails, a bloody mess. What will you bring me on a plate? It's so pleasant nibbling green things in the water. A clean world.

"Ginnie. I'm going to bring you something to eat. Sit up."

Silly crow-man. Come, dive into the water and lose your heavy boots. One by one they'll fall into the silt. You can float too, turning in wide circles, what was that poem? The falcon cannot hear the falconer, the fish turn round in green water.

Virginia rose out of the water to find herself in the old house in Philadelphia. She saw herself in the mirror, a lithe girl with blonde hair curling below her shoulders. Perne in a gyre, she said, and falconer. She had a good memory. As soon as she had learnt one poem, Father would give her another. Here's a good one, he said, and the page swam toward her.

"Here." A cool object touched her hands. "Here's a plate with cheese on it, and some crackers. Snap out of it, Gin, and sit up and eat."

Here's a good one. Open up. And she felt the plate turn into paper.

"I'm not hungry."

"God damn it, Ginnie, you've got to eat." Charles held something to her nose. It smelled like sour sheets. Virginia moved her head, but the smell followed. How could Charles do this? She tried to slip into the water world again, but it looked darker and more muddy. Her stomach began to heave like a boat pitched in a storm.

"Stop it," she heard herself say, but her voice sounded small and strange. She waved her hands in front of her and one of them collided with something hard. She heard a thud and felt the bed rise as Charles stood up.

"Ginnie." His hand grasped her arm, and the water heaved and roiled about her. I am caught, idiot fisherman, and she felt herself pulled up, up through the green water. Bursting to the surface, she felt the water inside her making her dizzy. She could not breathe in this thin air. Her gills shuddered.

The water inside her rose high and higher, and she heard

89

a low rasping sound, like thunder before a storm, and then she felt the water rise into her throat, a whole lake in her throat, and she gagged, holding it back, but it came into her mouth and she became a sluice, an opening for the flood. An arm held her roughly by the stomach, and she bent over, heaving. Minnows and muck, fish-eggs and thick weeds, rose up, and a little fish too, no longer iridescent but muddy, with a pale belly.

The arm half-pushed and half-lifted her back to the bed. Her body felt light and thin, a fish cleaned and scraped, drying on a rock in the sun. She heard Charles moving about, sloshing water in a bowl, his breathing labored and his knees cracking as he bent to the carpet. Near he seemed now, and she could imagine each crease in his trousers, and the movement of his shoulders as he worked. Virginia's head began to hurt, a harsh, dry hurt, and her mouth felt parched, although the thought of a glass of water, held by Charles's hand to her mouth, made the lake seem to roil again.

Arms lifted her, to move her under something soft, and the air fanned her face as something floated over her. She heard Charles go out of the room and down the stairs, and soon she heard him talking on the phone to someone, his voice a dull murmur.

X. Ducklings

"'Mr. and Mrs. Mallard were looking for a place to live,'" began Rose. It was Monday night. She was curled up on the middle of the children's bed, between Sophie and Elizabeth. Their hair was still wet from the bath, and Rose felt the wetness on both of her shoulders, through her kimono, where they leaned into her.

"'But every time Mr. Mallard saw what looked like a nice place, Mrs. Mallard said it was no good. There were sure to be foxes in the woods or turtles in the water, and she was not going to raise a family where there might be foxes or turtles. So they flew on and on.'"

"I saw a turtle today, at Bushy Hill," said Sophie.

"Shush, Sophie." Elizabeth moved closer to Rose.

"The turtle was this big." Sophie held her hands up in the air to shape a shell. "And it was green and black."

"Mmm," said Rose.

Elizabeth nudged Rose. She began to read again. What a magnificent book, she thought. I would be content if mine could be half as good. If only I could draw.

"Why?" asked Sophie.

Rose looked at the pages she had just read. The ducks' tails waved above the water of the pond in the Public Garden.

"Why do they look in the mud, you mean?" Rose asked.

"No, why didn't they find much?"

"Oh, Sophie," said Elizabeth. "There just wasn't much to find."

"They could find worms," said Sophie in a small voice.

"Maybe it was a city pond," offered Rose, "and fish and worms didn't like it so much."

"But ducks like it."

Elizabeth sat up straight and glared.

"We're reading now, Sophie, try just to listen. Elizabeth wants to hear the story."

As their heads sank back into her shoulders, Rose read, and the sepia colors of the book and the familiar words buoyed her up. She had walked the ten blocks to the creek with Hallie, and ten blocks back, and even though she'd slept on the bank, she'd woken up feeling drowsy and disoriented. I'll go to bed soon, she promised herself, peering at the children's lamb clock. 8:30 now. I can be in bed by 9:00 if I wish, and a sensation of sleep folded over her now like an immense wing. The feathers settled, as Rose read in a half-dream, and in the midst of this lull the baby began to roll and push. Rose felt a kick in her ribs, and another one, and then she saw her whole belly waving gaily under her kimono as the baby bumped and turned. A sharper sensation in her bladder, from a butting in that direction, hurt, and she placed her hand under the middle of her belly, pushing up.

"'Look out!' squawked Mrs. Mallard, all of a dither.'"

And what would this birth be like? Rose thought of stories she had collected through the years, of women bending to take out the laundry and finding the baby slipping between their legs, or feeling a little indigestion after supper, and ten minutes later giving one push. Sophie's birth had been much quicker than Elizabeth's—the pain had become terrible only two and a half hours before Sophie emerged, and Rose had only pushed for twenty minutes— but Rose had taken no medication, and when she finally asked for it, the nurse had said, Sorry, it's too late. She could still remember her terror in the last few minutes of her labor—transition, they called it, but it felt like agony. Those contractions had shaken her to her very core, as if she were a city being bombed, and nothing that William or the nurse could do or say had reassured her. How could this baby be born? she had thought, how could it live through this, and Rose too? William had made her furious, sounding so encouraging, as if this were a celebration and not a strange and terrifying grief.

But Rose pictured again Sophie's small body, and the way the whole room had become brighter and warmer, a pleasant place, as they lay the baby on her chest and she touched her fingers, all wrinkly and curled up, and her puckered face, with the mouth already making sucking

93

motions. All that happened after that—the pushing out of her placenta, the stitches, the kneading of her uterus—had been painful but marginal, fused along the edges of a luxurious blur filled only with the baby's tininess. And it had been the same with Elizabeth's birth: her soft weight, her funny head, had astonished Rose.

"I can say the names," said Sophie. "Jack, Kack, Lack . . . um, Quack . . ."

"Mack," added Elizabeth.

"Don't tell me. Mack . . ."

"What's the letter that comes after M?" Elizabeth hinted, trying to be patient.

"A, B, C, D, E, F, G . . ." Sophie whispered her letters. "N. Nack. Is that all?"

"Almost," said Rose.

"Whisper the others."

Rose whispered, and Sophie told them, and Rose continued, thinking, so many ducklings, and I'm overwhelmed by the thought of a third, with Sophie and Elizabeth already so big, Sophie almost in Kindergarten.

Just as the Irish policeman in the book came running to help Mrs. Mallard and her brood cross the street, Rose heard the phone ring, and a moment later William poked his head around the door.

"Phone's for you. Hallie."

"Don't go!" cried Sophie.

"I'll call her back very soon," said Rose, and William disappeared.

Rose followed Mrs. Mallard and her seven children to Charles Street and then across Beacon, "'right on into the Public Garden,'" as Elizabeth said roundly, proud of her reading. Such a satisfying conclusion, thought Rose, for there was Mr. Mallard waiting, and the island, and the swan boats, and the peanuts, and a delightful life ahead of them all. She lingered on the last picture, each duck a silhouette, with restful shadows from the bridge and the trees, and from each duckling. Elizabeth and Sophie gazed at the picture too. Quietly Rose sighed and closed the book. William appeared again in the doorway. Rose kissed the children and turned off the lamp as William came in to say goodnight.

Opening the door to her study, Rose saw the pages of her story—the one with the figure like her mother in it—scattered on her desk in the dusky light. She could almost feel the characters looking at her, one or two of them impatient, waiting for her to write down their words.

Hallie told Rose about her mother. Listening, Rose sat on the edge of her desk and gazed at the garden. The world seemed to tremble. "My mother," Hallie was saying, and it took Rose a moment to understand. Her mother was in the hospital. She had taken pills.

Elizabeth called, "Mommy!" and Rose promised, "I'll be there in a moment."

Sitting on the children's bed after settling Elizabeth down again, Rose thought of Hallie this afternoon as they had folded up the blanket. She had looked worried, but she had said so little. Her mother was low, Hallie had said, shrugging her shoulders, and Rose had felt hesitant about asking more questions. What could I have done? Rose asked in her own defense. She saw Hallie sometimes as a house with drawn curtains, in which someone comes to a window and pulls a curtain aside, and you can see the room lit up behind them just for a moment, and they begin to open the window as if to call to you, but then they stop, and move away, and all you can see is light and maybe the corner of an armchair. But how could I not know what her house is like?

Of course she had known some things from childhood, how you had to be very quiet when you played at Hallie's, especially in the afternoon, and also in the morning if you slept over. Hallie always made breakfast for herself, and lunch too, which had impressed Rose, for her own mother had often appeared to live in the kitchen, and Rose would never have thought of making a sandwich for herself until she was much older and beginning to feel babied.

"Can babies choke?" Sophie's voice floated out from

her pillow. Rose started, and looked over at the faint moon of Sophie's face.

"I thought you were asleep."

"I can't sleep."

"How do you come to think about babies choking?" Rose went to Sophie's side of the bed and sat down. She drew her finger along Sophie's nose.

"I don't know. Can they? If they're on their tummy? A girl at Bushy Hill said you have to be careful, and babies have to sleep on their sides. She said we'd better be careful about our baby."

Rose felt irritated toward this messenger of Bushy Hill. Children learned so quickly how to needle each other, how to turn someone else's good news into distress. "You don't need to worry, Sophie, we'll be careful. And anyway, babies are very sturdy. Most babies don't choke if they lie on their tummy."

"What if they lie that way a long time, and no one knows? Would they die?"

"I'm sure they'd be fine, Sophie. Now get to sleep." Oh, God, thought Rose, I hope they'd be fine. She felt how easy it was to belong to the society of grown-ups, who smile and smile, pretending the goodness of the world in front of children. Rose wished to be truthful. Looking at Sophie now, whose eyes were still open gazing at Rose, she thought, I will spare you what I can, and I hope ardently that you always believe in the possibility of goodness.

Sophie sighed and turned onto her side. Rose drew up the sheet and rubbed her back until she could hear Sophie's breathing becoming deep and regular. A familiar memory came to her, of standing with Hallie on the edge of the college pond—they must have been seven or eight—and poking sticks into the water. A skinny man with a tanned and wrinkled face and bow-legs had emerged from under the trees to stand near them and watch as they tied string to their sticks—Rose had had the idea to catch a fish. He looked at them intently, his blue eyes crinkled and puzzled-looking, or maybe thoughtful, and Rose's scalp had seemed to rise an inch off her head, and a wind had seemed to blow inside. Let's go, she had whispered to Hallie, but Hallie had stood there, staring at her fishing pole, as if she hadn't heard. Hallie, Rose had said softly, tugging at Hallie's t-shirt, let's go now. It was then that she had looked into Hallie's face, to see a panic of such immensity in Hallie's eyes that for a moment Rose felt abandoned. She clutched Hallie's arm hard and shook her. You've got to run with me now, she said, as she pulled Hallie after her, past the man with the strange half-smile on his face and the brown forearms with slight bulges, like Popeye's. Hallie had run behind her and had started to sob, Rose, wait. They had run to Rose's bike and Rose had scraped her shin on the wheel trying to jump on, and Hallie had slipped off the back twice as Rose had started up, and slowly, slowly, Rose had pedalled and the bike had wavered down the road until they saw the tennis courts and, a few blocks later, the elementary school. Hallie held tight to Rose, all the way home.

Rose could not remember talking about the incident again, and for years afterwards she and Hallie had stayed away from the pond, but that man had often come into Rose's thoughts. Maybe he had been an ordinary person, interested in their game. Maybe he had been poor, or from another town, and had stopped his truck for a moment to have a look at the pond on a hot day. But even now she remembered the cold air on her head and her feeling of something vicious about to rend the world.

Rose stood up and smoothed the covers over Sophie and Elizabeth. She pulled the curtain a couple of inches to keep out the light from the street, and then she went downstairs. Looking through the kitchen window, she saw William on the back porch, sitting at the top of the steps, reading the newspaper in the porch light. Rose opened the screen door and sat near him, her kimono folded under her knees. A few fireflies hovered and darted above the garden.

William folded the paper. "I think I'll get up earlier tomorrow."

"Mm," Rose said. She tried to think how to tell William about Hallie's mother, how she lay tonight in a hospital bed.

"I can almost see my way to finishing this book before the baby comes."

Rose nodded. She hoped he could finish it, because she would need his help in August. He was writing about Egypt, and his subject seemed to branch out and become larger and larger, so that sometimes she worried the book would never be done. Rose often gazed at the pictures William had in his study, of the pyramids and the Nile, taken by American travellers to Egypt a hundred years ago. Even Henry Adams had been there. Rose thought of Adams's wife, a photographer. She'd committed suicide a few years after that visit, Rose remembered. She'd drunk something, hadn't she? Something for developing photographs? William was writing the last chapter now, about Mary Cassatt. He said she found the pyramids and tombs abhorrent and compelling, because they seemed to crush her own art, make it seem small and insignificant by comparison. William said Cassatt's brother had grown very ill on that vacation, and Cassatt had had a nervous breakdown afterward.

Rose could smell the mint and the chives near the porch, and she could see the honeysuckle glimmering in the hedge. William touched his ear and then patted his shirt pocket, a habit of his ever since he'd given up smoking, when Elizabeth was born. He seemed always to be hoping he'd find one last cigarette there, by some miracle.

"So Hallie's going back to New York tomorrow?"

"Actually, no."

William raised his eyebrows.

"Her mother's in the hospital." Rose paused. "Apparently she took an overdose of sleeping pills."

"You're kidding."

"I'm not kidding."

William rubbed both hands on his face. He made a long, low sigh, like a whistle. Then he leaned his face on his hands and looked at Rose.

"Why'd she do that?"

"I don't know." Rose thought about how Hallie's

mother had sometimes appeared in the middle of the day, in her slip, when she and Hallie would be playing in Hallie's room. Once Rose had thought she was a ghost.

"I guess she's been unhappy," she said.

"It's strange, but Hallie seems that way to me."

"What way?"

"Unhappy."

"Well, she's had things to be unhappy about."

William looked down at the paper.

Rose pressed him. "Do you think she really seemed that unhappy on Saturday?"

William rubbed his hand over his mouth.

"Yes."

"How?"

He swatted a mosquito on his arm. "I thought she seemed as if she was looking for something."

Rose felt suddenly jealous, as if William had a more intimate understanding of Hallie than she did. She hadn't noticed anything new about Hallie on Saturday, or today either. Now that she thought about it, William had seemed almost flirtatious with Hallie, cocking his head, talking about the meaning of life or whatever.

"Maybe she was looking for a good-looking man to talk philosophy with."

William snorted. "Thank you for the compliment."

Rose tried to think of something biting to say. William always made her feel ridiculous for her jealousy. But she knew how he loved talking to women. She herself loved talking to Hallie. And how could you be sure what was just talk, and what was threaded through with something else?

A child's voice called from upstairs.

"Mommy."

Rose sighed and pushed herself up. She avoided looking at William, as she opened the screen door into the kitchen and let it close with a soft bang.

Sophie stood at the top of the stairs, her nightgown small and dusky white. "I just remembered, I left my swimsuit in the car. It's wet."

"I'll hang it up," said Rose. "Go back to bed, Sophie, it's getting late."

"Am I going to Bushy Hill tomorrow?"

"Yes, Sophie."

"Is Elizabeth going too?"

"Yes. Of course she is. You're going together."

"Is it raining?"

"No, it's not raining."

"If it rains we can't swim."

"I think you'll be able to swim. Now go to bed."

Sophie mumbled goodnight, and Rose walked into the living room to turn off the light.

XI. Hospital

Virginia opened her eyes to see Charles sitting in an orange plastic chair. He looked disheveled, his shirt rumpled, his shoulders sagging.

"Were you asleep?" he asked.

"I can't possibly sleep here, Charles. I've got the damn nurses coming in every five seconds to take my pulse and make sure the needle's still stuck in the same place."

"I'm sorry." Charles looked bewildered, as if he'd walked into the wrong room.

"You should be sorry. I have no idea why you called the doctor in the first place, and now this." Virginia felt that she would cry.

"Ginnie." Charles leaned toward her. "I couldn't wake you up yesterday."

"You woke me up. You made me throw up, you shook me so hard."

Charles sighed and looked away. With faint surprise, Virginia noticed a vase full of flowers.

"You took too many pills."

"What do you know about it? I took as many pills as I needed."

"What the hell were you doing?" Charles flushed. "You could have died."

Virginia slowly remembered the fish-eggs and the water, the little fish swimming in circles.

"I was just sleepy."

"Sleepy! Ginnie! You took most of a bottle. They had to pump out your stomach."

Shards, like bits of ice, splintered, came back, each melting into a fragment of something: white coats, someone holding her wrist, a nurse with a needle, a hospital room like a salmon-colored box, its edges bloated.

"I . ."

"What?"

"I think I just took a few, Charles. I couldn't sleep. I needed something more to help me sleep."

"You sleep all the time. Sleep is not the problem."

102

"Oh, you're so sure what the problem is. What do you know about it?"

Charles bent his head into his hands, covering his face. For a moment she thought he was laughing. His shoulders shook, and she felt like slapping him, until she heard the noise, childish and tired. For a moment she thought of touching his shoulders, saying It's all right, as she had said to Hallie once, stroking her hair, when she woke in a thunderstorm.

"Charles."

He looked up, and she felt surprised at his silver hair and the wrinkles on his face, the loose flesh under his chin. His eyes looked injured.

"I'm sorry," she said.

Charles gazed at Virginia, and it seemed to her for a moment that her whole life with him hung in the air between them: their wedding and honeymoon, Hallie's birth, luxurious Saturday mornings in bed while the baby slept, Charles's doctoring, the messy house, a white coffin, and then a dusky evening in a garden with a mouth on hers, not Charles's, and arms around her, not Charles's, and a moon winking, not the moon she'd ever known. And Hallie growing shyer and more secretive, her face pinched and worried, and the old house packed up, and the new house a pretty shell into which to pour her life, only now her life seemed limp and worthless.

Someone knocked softly at the door.

"Can I come in?"

It was Hallie. Her hair looked like a different color, more burnished. Her eyes looked dark. She carried a little tray.

Virginia drew the sheets more closely around her. She put a hand to her own hair and felt its thinness. She had had such thick hair when Hallie was a baby.

"I brought you a muffin, if you'd like. The cafeteria actually looked good." Hallie placed the tray carefully on the hospital table to the side of the orange chair.

Virginia felt queasy. "I'm on a liquid diet at the

moment." She tried to smile, but she felt as if her face had become dry, almost cemented, so that it might crack. "I can't bear hospitals."

Hallie looked at her. "I guess you haven't been in one since my birth."

Something dry, like a small leaf, seemed to lodge in Virginia's throat, and she tried to cough. For a moment she thought she would choke. Charles stood up and bent over her.

"Ginnie? Are you O.K.?" His face looked furrowed.

Virginia motioned toward the plastic water jug, and Charles poured her a cup of water. He raised her bed a little so she could drink. Her hand trembled.

The water felt cool. Virginia looked at the flowers. A crimson rose stood among daisies and sprays of tiny white flowers. She closed her eyes.

Her labor with Hallie had been frightening, a blur of pain, nurses' faces looming, fingers thrusting between her legs, hurting, measuring, and some woman in another room screaming Jesus Mary and Joseph Jesus Mary and Joseph. At some point before morning they had given her something, and all she remembered after that was a nurse bursting into her room, and sticking her blotchy face into Virginia's, saying, Did we have our baby? and Virginia, woozy from the drugs, trying to remember, did I? The nurse laughed at Virginia's confusion. Soon she rolled in a little bed with a white object on it, an angry, tiny red face at the top like a monkey's, its mouth open, shrieking. How can that possibly be mine? Virginia had thought.

Life is a horror. To be a woman is a horror. And when Charles was finally allowed to see her, he brought a bunch of daffodils and held them out to her, his face looking innocent and happy. He could have no idea, even though he was a doctor. And later, once she came home, off he would go each morning, looking cheerful and ready for his patients, and she would be staring at the egg on the counter, and his coffee cup with the grounds at the bottom, and Hallie would be crying to be fed.

Virginia opened her eyes. Hallie sat at the foot of the bed, looking at her.

"Were you talking to me?" Virginia asked.

Hallie shook her head. "Could I get you something?" she asked.

Virginia thought. What could this hospital hold, for her?

"Another cup of water?" Hallie pointed to the water jug.

"Yes."

Hallie poured the water carefully. She handed it to Virginia.

Even as a little girl, Hallie had brought her things: a cup of milk, a piece of bread with jam spread in thick, childish waves, a dandelion. She would approach Virginia solemnly, and hold out her hand with whatever it was. And once things got too hard, and the house seemed to darken and close in, Hallie would wait for her. Once Virginia discovered her sitting in the hallway just outside her bedroom. It must have been mid-morning, because the sun had beaten on the shades of her room. Virginia had just woken up, and stepped into the hallway to see Hallie in her blue nightgown with the lace around the hem. She must have been two, because her cheeks still looked plump and babyish. For you, she said, offering Virginia a sticky pile of papers, colored all over in scribbles. Virginia remembered kneeling beside her then, and catching her in her arms. She was so little, to be patient in that way.

Virginia noticed Hallie's silver earrings. They looked like drops of water. Hallie sat on the bed with her hands folded.

"You're going back to New York?"

"Actually, I thought I'd stay a few more days. Until you felt better."

How thin she was, thought Virginia. Hallie's waist looked as slender as a girl's. She hadn't had a baby, that was why, and here she was, thirty-seven. What had happened? She'd written them about her two miscarriages. But it was hard to talk about such things. Looking at Hallie now, as she sat soberly on the bed, Virginia suddenly thought, maybe she's had more of them and she can't bring herself to tell us. And Morey—what was Hallie's life like with him? Virginia barely knew him.

"Hallie?"

"Yes?" Hallie looked at her.   But   how   could Virginia begin to talk about things like that? She glanced at Charles, who seemed to be studying his hands.

"Are you still hoping—I mean . . . you and Morey . . .." Virginia waved her hand in the general direction of Hallie's torso.

"I can always hope." Hallie looked at her, and then looked away.

And what more is there to say? thought Virginia. At least Hallie had borne her loss early. She had not had to wait nine months, and all through an excruciating labor and delivery, only to see her baby blue from lack of oxygen, the cord around its neck. A beautiful baby, perfectly all right except that it could not breathe, baffled in making its way from that wet world, inside, to this dry and painful place. Such things could happen.

Virginia felt a touch on her shoulder.

"I'm just going to walk around a little," Hallie said. She looked sad as she stood up and turned to go. Have I said something? thought Virginia. Have I hurt her feelings? Hallie walked out into the corridor and was gone.

Charles was now studying his shoes. Virginia could picture them, his doctor shoes she called them, the reddish-brown ones with the tiny holes sprinkled around the toe. He looked up, but Virginia closed her eyes. I cannot bear to talk again, she thought.

Charles cleared his throat. "I need to step out for a moment too, Gin. Will you be all right for two minutes?" Charles pushed himself out of the orange chair with both arms, swaying a little as he tried to gain his balance.

Virginia felt suddenly small. As Charles too vanished into the corridor, her chest came alive, as if someone invisible pricked her with a thousand tiny pins. I can't breathe, she thought, for the pins seemed to pierce her lungs and her heart, making blood fill her rib cage. Don't go, she thought. Don't leave me here. I'm afraid of this bright light and these nurses. I'm afraid of needles and of the door opening. Who can hold me safe from this terror?

XII. Fish

In the bathroom near the visitors' lounge Hallie sat folded over. Her stomach felt as if it stretched tightly around a fist, and her forehead felt cold and sweaty. A woman was in the stall next to her. She could see the woman's shoes, dull black pumps into which plump feet were squeezed, and she could hear the woman breathing heavily, pulling paper off the roll. The woman stood up, making the seat bump, and the toilet flushed loudly. In a moment the woman pushed the stall door open and wheezed over to the sink. Hallie heard water running, and then paper towels being pulled. After another minute or so, the pumps moved across the floor and the door swung open on heavy hinges.

Hallie thought about how frail her mother looked today in the small hospital bed, as if her bones had become dry and light. The door to the bathroom swung open and another woman walked quickly across the tiled floor. Her sandals were flat with tiny plastic beads along the thong, and her feet looked slender, chocolate brown. She placed her large leather bag on the stall floor and Hallie could hear her rummaging in it. A musical sound of trickling water came, and then a sound of paper tearing. Hallie gazed at the walls of her stall. She could see herself in the shiny surface of the paper dispenser. Above her head, near the top of the door, a little sign had been glued: Dial 911 for Emergency. The walls had been scrubbed clean, although Hallie could read traces of graffitti: "Joe F.," someone had written, and "suck." Initials had been scrawled inside a heart: "H.M." and "S.G."

The scrawls made her uncomfortable, and in a rush a memory besieged her, of a hot summer day she hadn't thought of in years. It was a day when she and Rose had decided to go to the little pond where tadpoles hovered, ink drops, at the edge and then darted away all together, and a thick green scum clouded the water. Rose found two good sticks, long and smooth, and Hallie helped her tie strings to the ends. We need worms, Rose said, but Hallie said she thought the fish might be hungry enough to eat just string.

It had been fun standing next to Rose watching the bit of string touch the water and looking at the beautiful trees on the other side.

How had she first known to be frightened? Suddenly the whole place changed, as if a storm had come up, the trees growing darker, and yet the sky remained pale blue. She felt him before she saw him, felt his intention, his eyes on her bare legs, her shorts, and once she looked at him, his crazy eyes, the smooth tan skin of his temples, she knew how he wanted to bend her to the ground, to hold her arms, to hurt her, because she was small and pretty and he had something broken in his head, and prettiness was something he could not understand, and the only way he could get close to it was to hurt it. She could do nothing, she knew, anticipating only the moment when her elbows would scrape dirt, and the pond and the trees would turn upside down, tearing a gash in the sky.

It was Rose who saved her, shouting something and pulling at her roughly, although her feet had become planted until Rose tore out the roots, and Hallie discovered she could run on stumps. Surely his arm would swing out and capture her, surely he would take giant steps and bring her back to the pond's edge to be thrust down, but Rose held her elbow, pulling, until magically, as in a dream, they reached her bike and Hallie could not believe that she managed to stay on the back, and the bike wavered and moved forward, and Rose pumped, and no arm reached them, until houses went by and a child on a tricycle, and regular people, and, after a hundred houses or more, and dozens of crosswalks, they reached Rose's porch. Up the stairs they ran, to Rose's and Catherine's room, and they shut the door and looked out the window. Could he follow us? Hallie asked, again and again, and Rose assured her that they were safe, her mother downstairs doing the laundry, Catherine braiding her friend's hair on the porch. He was probably just looking at the pond, anyway, Rose said, and Hallie had been grateful for the lie. Of course Rose had known, she must have, how close the world had come to shattering. Hallie had tried not to let Rose see how she kept glancing outside, for Rose was brave, a hero, just like in a story, and Hallie held to her.

Hallie studied the little squares of linoleum beneath her feet. The world could break in so many ways. Children always thought their mothers held it together. Hallie felt ill and furious at once. How could her mother wish herself out of life? It was as if all Hallie's tiptoeing as a child, her attempt to be good and helpful, had come to nothing.

The bathroom door burst open and in ran a little girl, laughing.

"Lucy Goosey," a woman said mildly. Her voice sounded like water rushing over pebbles. The little girl gave a squeal of delight and banged the stall door shut.

"I'm in here!" she said. "I'm going." Hallie could just barely see a little shoe a foot off the floor.

"That's fine," said the woman. "I'll wait for you."

"I bet you don't know which toilet I'm in."

"Goodness," said the woman. "I can't guess."

"This one!" said the girl, and she let her plastic shoe fall off onto the floor just under the stall door.

"Lucy!" the woman said. "Put your shoe back on, missie."

Lucy laughed and flushed her toilet. Hallie saw a little bare foot slip into the shoe, and she heard the door bang as the girl jumped out.

"Wash hands," said the woman.

As the little girl and her companion opened the door and the girl hopped out, Hallie sat up and held her elbows. The fluorescent lights in the ceiling hummed. She stood up slowly and turned to flush the toilet. In the mirror, as she washed her hands, she saw her hair lying flat, her lips pale. She looked for her lip pencil and traced the outline of her mouth in a bright color (raspberry, she read in gold letters on the pencil's side), then dipped her finger into the little pot of gloss. She brushed her hair, and the face in the mirror began to look a little better. Her blue shirt had a stain on it, maybe from tea, and she held a paper towel under cold water, then rubbed hard. The stain began to fade, but her shirt had a deep blue patch of wetness. As she straightened up, she felt the shirt cling damply to her stomach.

In the lounge, Hallie hesitated. She riffled through the magazines—*Sports Illustrated, Time, People, Highlights for Children*—and she chose an old *New Yorker*, but when she had found a seat by a large rubber plant and opened the pages she could not read.

A lady in a light blue pant-suit sat almost opposite from her. She was thick-set, her legs as round as trees. Her cheeks had soft folds, and her neck continued them. She was knitting something with yellow yarn that emerged out of a big embroidered bag.

"Grandma." The little girl with the plastic shoes jumped over to the woman.

"Wait, honey, I'm counting stitches." She whistled a little as she counted, and the little girl shifted from one foot to the other, scratching her head. When the woman looked up and said "Alright, missie," the little girl almost shouted, "There's a new fish! A gold one! Come see it!" and she pulled her grandmother's fleshy arm until the woman seemed to roll herself out of the chair. The girl pulled her over to a huge fish tank. You could see through it to the other side, where another child was peering, and from this distance Hallie could see pretend seaweed and a wrecked ship with holes big enough for fish to swim through.

The little girl was hopping up and down in front of the tank, pointing above her head. Hallie squinted, and thought she saw a golden shape, almost circular. The grandmother bent toward the girl, yellow yarn trailing out of the bag on her arm. The girl tapped on the glass and waved to the fish. Hallie glimpsed one with red stripes, and two orange ones.

Hallie looked back at the magazine, rubbing the glossy pages between her thumb and index finger. The images looked silly to her, a jumble of letters, an eye, a forehead, a bottle. She wished for white paper, the openness and simplicity of a new sheet. Where's my sketchbook? she wondered, opening her bag. Her hands trembled as she searched, sifting through pens and pencils, lipsticks,

Kleenex, keys. She remembered putting it on the bedstand just before she'd turned off the light last night. She'd opened it, to try a sketch of the quilt folded at the end of the bed, its curves and softness reminding her of a seashell somehow, or a wave. Damn, she thought, I forgot to bring it. She looked up to see the grandmother rolling back into her seat, and the little girl jumping from foot to foot and looking straight at Hallie.

"There's a new fish," the girl offered.

"Oh." Hallie couldn't think what to say.

"It's yellow. A yellow fish."

"Mmm."

"I know all the fish."

"You do?" Hallie held her finger in her magazine.

"I come here every day. Yesterday the purple fish was gone. I think it died." She looked at Hallie as if with a question.

"Oh. That's too bad." Hallie fiddled with her watch, turning it round and round her wrist.

"There's ten fish now."

"All right, missie, let the lady read her magazine," the grandmother said. She had put her glasses on to look more closely at her stitches. She glanced at Hallie shyly, a small smile glimmering at the corners of her mouth. When Hallie smiled back, she ventured, "Lucy loves fish."

"I'm going to have my own fish one day soon. I'm going to have four fish, or maybe five. A tiger fish, and a purple one too."

"Maybe for Christmas," said her grandmother.

"Sooner than Christmas," said Lucy, "because I have five dollars already. And I can feed them myself. You just put in a tiny pinch." She held her fingers in the air to show Hallie. "My mother lives in this hospital," Lucy added. "We come to this part to see the fish."

"Oh," Hallie said. My mother too, she wished to say.

Lucy looked at her for a long moment, and then opened her grandmother's bag. She pulled out paper and crayons. "I'll draw you a picture of the fish." She put the paper on a chair and kneeled on the floor to draw. Hallie watched her make a big shape, filling the whole space. The outline was orange, and inside was an explosion of bright yellow. The eye was purple. When she was done, she wrote in black letters at the bottom, very carefully, Lucille Mabel Anne.

"How do you spell your name?" she asked Hallie, and as Hallie told her each letter she printed it painstakingly in the upper left corner, just above the fish's head.

"Here," she said proudly, holding out the paper to Hallie.

"Thank you," said Hallie. "You're a good artist."

"I know." Lucy sighed and put back the crayons. Something about the small sturdiness of her shoulders made Hallie wish to catch her up and hold her, bring her home on the airplane. Look what I caught! she could say to Morey. Some fish! he would say, holding Lucy up in the air and twirling. Lucy opened a pack of lifesavers and popped a red one into her mouth.

"Want one?" she asked, holding the pack open in her palm.

The paper was torn around the opening. A green one was next. Lime.

"Thank you," said Hallie, as she unstuck it from the yellow one underneath. In her mouth the candy was hard and sour, with little ridges on one side where the letters were. As a child, her favorite had been red, and Rose's had been green.

Hallie stirred herself to gather up her purse and the drawing and rise.

"Are you going home?" Lucy looked up at Hallie.

Could you come, could you come with me, Hallie thought in a sing-song, picturing how she could tuck Lucy into bed and read colorful picture books to her, and how on Sundays she and Morey could take her to the park.

"Not quite yet," she said. "I have someone to visit." As she smoothed her skirt, she added, "Thank you for the picture."

Lucy nodded. Hallie made her way between the rows of chairs and people's legs. As she reached the wide doors into the hallway, she turned. A gay little hand shot up from the seat next to the rubber plant, as Lucy waved, her face wreathed in smiles.

Entering the hallway, Hallie saw a bank of telephones against the wall. A young woman with straggly hair was on one of them, her face intent and sober, her head leaning against the divider. She was surreptitiously smoking a cigarette and tapping the ashes into an empty pack. Hallie stared at her for a moment, watching the smoke make a cloud around the woman's phone, and the woman seemed to notice, for the next moment she stubbed out the cigarette against the metal shelf under the phone and turned her back to Hallie. I should call Morey, Hallie thought. He must be at work by now. She pictured his drafting table near the huge window looking across the city, his fine drawing, the straight pencil lines and the tiny numbers and letters along the edges. She wondered if he knew how those careful lines and numbers had soothed her, and inspired her too. Morey was modest about his work. It's nothing like art, he used to say, but she'd shake her head and say, Look at the gorgeousness of this design. I think it looks good, too, Hallie, but it's not the same thing as art. Sometimes she urged him to go back to his painting. He'd done magnificent things at school, before he'd gone over to architecture; Hallie had been jealous. But it was Hallie who'd stuck with her painting, stubbornly, her love of color and line growing, in spite of the fact that she'd never drawn as much attention as Morey had. She often thought he must miss it all, feel disappointment.

"Hello?" Morey's voice sounded husky.

"Hello." Hallie studied the metal backing to which the phone was attached.

"Hallie? Is that you?"

"Yes, I . ."

"Are you calling from the airport?"

"I . . . No, I'm still in Ohio."

The other woman hung up her phone and bent to look into a small suitcase, her hair flopping over her face and hanging in weedy tendrils in the air. Something stung Hallie's eyes and made her throat tighten. She rubbed the back of her hand against her eyes and her cheeks again and again, but her face had become slippery and her nose had begun to run.

"I'm sorry," she said thickly.

She could not hear Morey's words. The hospital itself seemed to dissolve around her, the hallway a wavering nebula, the people composed of watercolors. I will dissolve, she thought, but she did not dissolve.

Something fluttered to the floor near her shoe. She looked at it as if from a great height, wondering at the oval yellow shape, the purple dot. Remembering the child's sturdy shoulders, Hallie caught herself up. The yellow fish gleamed, a clear thing, and slowly the clarity spread to Hallie's shoes, the tiled floor, the angled sunlight coming into the hallway from outside.

She told Morey then about her mother, even about the fragility of her mother's body, the way her hands looked beautiful and wrinkled against the sheet, and how she could look at Hallie so piercingly that Hallie felt a hole had been carved out of her temple, her forehead, her heart. She pictured each thing she said flying across fields and towns to him.

"I'm worried about you," Morey said.

Hallie watched an old lady in a wheelchair, being pushed by a nurse. Something in Morey's voice made her remember how he'd looked, after the last time, when he'd come to bed. He had eased himself onto the bed slowly, as if he might crumble into bones and dust.

"Morey?"

"Yes?"

"I do love you, you know."

Morey was quiet.

"Did you hear me?"

"Yes. I love you too."

"I want things to be—better."

"I know. I want that too."

Hallie looked at the dial, waiting for him to say more.
"Morey."
"Yes."
"About a baby."
"Don't worry about all that now, Hallie. You have enough going on there."
"I'm not worried, I just . . I think it might be possible."
The silence on the other end seemed to Hallie like a field, lying fallow.
"Did you hear me?"
Morey coughed. "I heard you, Hallie. You just handle things there, and come home safely."
"You'll think about it?"
"About a baby?"
"Yes."
"I always think about it."
"Could we do it?"
The question hung between them.
"Sure we could, pal, if you felt ready." He hadn't called her that for a long time.
"Maybe I should come out there," he added.
"It'll be all right. Thanks. I'll be home soon."
"I'm happy to come out there if you need me, Hal."
"I'll be O.K. I think my mother will be O.K."
After she hung up, Hallie stood quietly for a moment. Then she bent to look into her purse, and she found the piece of paper with a number scrawled on it. I'll call May, she had said to her father this morning. May would want to know.
Hearing the rings, Hallie tried to picture May's life in Florida. She lived in a condo near the water, she'd said once, when Hallie had called her around Easter one year. She walked on the beach often, collecting shells. She and Frank went to a lot of events together, luncheons and talks. May accepted so much that Hallie's mother disdained. Hallie remembered May wearing pink: a pink scarf around her neck, a pink blouse. She herself seemed much more vivid than pink. Hallie pictured flowered chairs, potted

118

plants, and French windows onto a little deck. May's old house, in Ohio, had been pretty and neat, a little gingerbread right on Linden Street. Hallie had known her since she was little. She'd enjoyed sitting on her porch, eating ice cream.

"Yes?" May's voice sounded wavery and far away.

"May?"

"Yes? Is this Ginnie?"

Hallie hesitated. "No, it's Hallie."

"Hallie! Darling! How are you! I hope everything's O.K.?"

"Well . . ."

"Tell me, are your mother and father all right?"

"Yes, they're all right, it's just . . Well, my mother. May?"

"Yes?"

"You remember how she always takes pills to sleep?"

"Oh, Hallie." There was a long silence. "Is that what happened? Is she all right?"

Hallie swallowed.

"She's in the hospital, but I think she'll be going home soon, in a few days. She needs to get her strength up."

The phone crackled, and Hallie could barely hear May. She pressed the phone hard against her ear.

" . . . you take care of yourself, darling. You tell your mother I'll be there. In less than a week. You'll tell her that, won't you, darling?"

"I'll tell her that. Thank you, May. You don't have to come up."

"Of course I do, darling. Your mother's a dear friend."

"Thank you, May. She'll be glad."

The phone crackled again, and Hallie thought she'd lost the connection, when she heard May say, ". . .she's had some sad things in her life, Hallie. I'm sure you know."

"Well . . ."

"She was always so grateful to have you. The other was hard for her, you know."

"The other?"

May was quiet.

"May. I'm sorry, you said 'the other'?"

"You know, the baby and all that. When you were little."

Hallie felt ill. "I'm sorry, May, I don't understand what you're saying."

May seemed to be thinking.

"What baby?" Hallie pressed her.

"You mean you don't know about that? Your mother and father never told you about that?"

"I don't know what you're talking about, May. My mother never mentioned a baby."

"Well, I don't want to tell you something your mother couldn't bring herself to tell you."

"Did she have another baby besides me, May?"

"Maybe you should ask your father about it, Hallie. I shouldn't have brought it up. It's just, I was so upset about your mother, and I thought . . ."

"Actually, May, I don't think I could ask my father about this. Not right now, anyway. I think it might help me to know."

"Well . . . I'm not sure, Hallie. This is a difficult enough time right now."

"Please, May. Just tell me something. Just give me an idea."

Hallie could hear a small whistling sound, maybe a sigh. "Well. You couldn't have been more than one and a half. Your mother was pregnant, and . . . the baby was born, only . . ."

Hallie tried to think. "I don't remember anything about that."

"The baby was stillborn, darling. No one could have done anything."

"Was it a boy or a girl?"

"It was a boy."

"But why wouldn't someone have told me?"

The line crackled.

"May?"

" . . . and she didn't want it mentioned. She was shattered."

"My mother?"

"I worried about her."

"I see."

"I'm sorry, Hallie. I thought you knew. I thought your mother or father would have told you by now."

Hallie tried to think what to say.

"You're very precious to them, Hallie."

"Thank you, May. I mean, yes. Thank you." Am I? she thought.

"Will you still be in Ohio when I come?"

"I guess it depends how things go."

"Well, thank you for telling me, darling. This must be very hard for you. I'm sorry about the—it wasn't right of me to mention it, especially right now."

"No, it's all right. Thank you, May."

Hallie paused outside her mother's door. She took her brush out of her purse and brushed her hair, and then she looked for a small mirror. The rims of her eyes looked red, and her mascara had run, creating dark brown smudges. She rubbed them out, and put on new lip pencil and lipstick. Her hands felt light and shaky.

Someone had turned off the overhead light in her mother's room, so that only the lights above the bed were on. The orange plastic chair sat empty. Her mother lay still, her eyes closed, her hands on top of the sheet. For a moment Hallie's heart seemed to fold over, until she could see her mother's chest moving. Hallie walked to the window and touched the blinds. Pulling the cord to let in some sun, she looked at the parking lot and a sidewalk, fringed with bushes and mulch. A couple of planters had been placed near the entrance to the hospital, and Hallie saw a thin showing of pink and white flowers. Impatiens? Rose would know.

"You're back."

Hallie turned to see her mother's eyes open. A glittering, anxious look came into her mother's face.

"I cannot bear this," she said tremulously. "I cannot bear being here one minute more."

Hallie couldn't think what to say.

"Where is your father?"

"I'm not sure. Do you want me to find him?" Hallie moved away from the window.

"No. No. Stay."

Hallie sat in the orange chair.

"Can I get you something? More water?"

"No. I'm all right."

Her mother looked nervous.

"Mom."

"Yes."

"About the pills."

Her mother shook her head.

"I just want to understand something."

Her mother looked at her. "What is there to understand?"

"Did you mean to—I mean, the pills. Did you wish to take so many?"

Her mother made a wry face, as if she might say something sharp, but instead she paused, as if considering Hallie's question. "I'm not sure. I'm not sure I knew how many I was taking. I've been taking more, these days, because it's so hard to fall asleep."

"But —" Hallie hesitated.

"You want to ask me, why was I taking sleeping pills at all?"

Hallie shifted in her chair. "Well, I do wonder. I worry about you. I worried about you before this even happened."

Her mother listened, her eyes on Hallie's face.

"I mean," Hallie added, "I know you always did."

"I didn't, always."

"Well, you always slept in the middle of the day."

"Lots of people do."

Hallie sighed.

"Hallie. I know what you're saying. It's just, I don't have any answers. I feel so tired, and I want to sleep so much. I'm just like that."

"But it isn't just tiredness."

Her mother gazed at her and sighed. "No. It isn't just tiredness."

"Maybe if you could talk to someone —"

Her mother shook her head and waved her hand in the air, as if to scatter cobwebs.

Hallie took a breath. "May told me something."

"You talked to May?"

Her mother looked at her hard. The hospital room began to feel to Hallie like a strange heart, holding them inside. She imagined how it held both of them in its movements, the systole and the diastole, the rushing of the blood into the heart's muscle, the rushing away.

"And she told you—"

Hallie looked at her hands.

"Oh, I don't know. She said a few things. She said to tell you she'd be up here soon, in a week or so."

Hallie studied her mother's face, to see how this registered. She thought she could see something like a smile, hovering about her mother's mouth and eyes, but in the next moment it vanished, like the wink of a lightning bug, when she used to catch them with Rose.

"What else did she say?"

"Oh." Hallie regretted bringing up her conversation with May.

"When did she say she'd be coming?"

"In less than a week."

"May's a trooper."

Hallie looked quickly at her mother and smiled. "Yes. She's a trooper."

"She always wanted a family," her mother added. "She had some experiences, just like you, a long time ago."

"You mean, she had miscarriages?"

"Oh, God, yes, one after another. It was terrible."

Hallie thought about how May would hug her, her plump arms warm, her skin smelling like soap. She looked at her mother.

"And you?"

"What?"

"Did you have anything like that happen?"

How sharp her mother's eyes could look. Hallie felt almost afraid.

"What makes you ask that?"

"Oh, nothing, just that you were talking about May, and I thought . . ."

"I never had any miscarriages."

Hallie fell quiet, looking at her hands. She yearned for her sketchbook. She thought about touching the paper with her finger. Paper held such promise.

"What did May tell you?"

"She . . . Oh, I don't know. She thought I knew something that I didn't."

A delicate light seemed to come into her mother's face.

"Oh," she said, gazing at Hallie.

Hallie waited.

"You mean about the baby."

Hallie nodded.

Her mother's eyes filled. "It was a long time ago, Hallie. I'm sorry May brought it up. She had no business doing that. What does it matter now?"

"I felt grateful to her. It helps me gain a better picture of things."

Her mother was quiet.

The heart of the room beat around them, holding them inside its salmon-pink walls.

XIII. Home

At home, on Saturday morning, Virginia listened to Charles clanging around in the kitchen. He had bought groceries. She had heard the car doors opening, the rustle of paper bags, and now she could hear the refrigerator door opening and shutting, and the sound of bottles and cans, as Hallie and Charles put things away.

Virginia eased herself to the side of the bed. Her toes touched the carpet, and then her bare feet, as she felt for her thongs. Slipping them on, she took a breath and stood up. Hallie had just vacuumed, and the room looked clean, almost ironed.

In the bathroom, Virginia brushed her teeth and drank water from a cup. Idly, she opened the medicine cabinet. Someone had cleaned the shelves, and created an order: aspirin and Tylenol on one shelf, dental floss and toothpaste on another, sunscreen, bandaids, antibiotic ointment on another. Opening the linen closet, she gazed at neat rows of towels, sheets, wash cloths, soap. The shelves looked wide and white. Of course Charles had thrown out her pills. Virginia felt a tremor inside, at the base of her stomach. She felt an urge to sleep. What if she couldn't sleep?

Virginia slipped back to her room and lay on the bed. The scent of coffee floated up the stairs. Maybe Charles was making real coffee, instead of instant. Usually he just opened a jar now, spooning out the brown powder, but when they had first been married, Virginia remembered, he had used the old coffee pot and a raw egg. The egg brought the grounds to the bottom, although a few floated into the black coffee to bring a grain of bitterness to your tongue. Sometimes she would make French toast, and she and Charles would sit at the kitchen table talking and eating, and drinking coffee. Often they would find the bed again, tumbling into it as they unbuttoned buttons. Charles had been ardent, his tongue curious and determined. He had been handsome too, his hair thick as it rubbed into her, his jaw raspy with a young man's stubble.

Virginia could hear one of the French windows open,

and someone walking on the patio. Hallie's voice rose into the air, a question.

"What kind of flower is this?"

She could hear Charles's voice, muffled, responding, although she couldn't hear his words.

And hello, someone had whispered to Virginia. It was in the Banfords' garden, a long time ago. Ian Banford had come outside with her for a smoke after dinner. Hello, he had said, nuzzling her. She had felt heady then, and reckless. His mouth tasted of Scotch and smoke. Let me just have this, just once, she had thought, and she had clung to him. Astonishment had been in the trees and the damp grass, and in the moon winking through the clouds. They had lain on the grass, the ground hard and bumpy beneath them.

Coming inside from the garden, her dress damp and wrinkled, she had caught a look on Claire's face. Claire had been serving coffee, and a cake. She was standing by the dining table, the pot in her hand, and as soon as she looked at Ian and Virginia in the doorway, she had flushed a mottled color in her cheeks, and her eyes had become sharp and bright. She stared at Ian then, her mouth pinched. Well, well, Charles had said in a grand drunken gesture, where have you two love-birds been? He would not have believed it, but Claire knew. She held the knowledge all her life, thought Virginia, and never let me forget it, her snobby English nose pinched and white, her eyes like little painted eggs. Hello, Ginnie, she would say whenever they saw each other, the picture of cordiality, with her sensible English shoes and her affected carelessness about what she wore, an old gardener's jacket, a ridiculous floppy hat, her hair in a messy bun as if she were Princess Margaret on her horse. And then the romance of her weak heart, giving out on her when she was just fifty. Even so, Ian didn't mourn long. Virginia remembered meeting his young wife by accident on Broadway, when they had come through to see about the house and to visit the Banford children, scattered over Ohio and Michigan and Pennsylvania by then. His new wife—

Laura—must have been younger even than Rose and Catherine; maybe she was about Hannah's age then, in her early twenties. She had looked at Virginia with cool indifference, flaunting her long brown legs and her slenderness. Even if she had known about Ian and Virginia, she looked as if she couldn't care less. She had made Virginia feel so old.

And why had Rose taken on that huge house, anyway? What on earth could have moved her to live in this town, and in the same house where her mother and father scratched out each other's eyes? She pictured how Ian would sit across the table from her in later years, making her feel sexy and forlorn at once. Because he never tried it again, not really. Once or twice they fumbled around in odd corners, and she could remember a Christmas party when she found herself kissing him passionately against the dresser in his bedroom upstairs, until one of his daughters—Rose, it might have been—had come to the door and said What are you doing with Mrs. Greaves, Daddy? and he had laughed, embarrassed, and knelt down beside her, saying Oh nothing, nothing, only talking together, and then he had taken the girl's hand and walked out into the hallway. When she had said goodbye to him and Claire, Charles stamping his feet in the cold on the porch, she had seen a look of apology on Ian's face, but what had the apology been for? Was it because he had started up again, or because he had walked into the hallway with his daughter and had not come back?

And where is Charles? she thought. The bed felt dry and hard, and she felt a sudden hunger for Charles's weight and flesh, his dampness and warmth. She imagined Charles at the door, a cup of coffee in his hand. How sharp and hot it would taste.

"Charles."

"Yes, Gin."

"Are you coming up?"

"I'll be right there." She listened to his footsteps, halting and tired, on the stairs. Coming into the room, he looked unsure of himself.

"Can I get you something, Ginnie?"

Virginia could not think what to say.

"Gin? Can I get you something?"

If Charles would sit on the bed, maybe hold her hand. I love you, he might say, a soft rasp in his voice, and she could almost imagine him a young man again, his jaw clean and angular, his eyes clear of the future. It is terrible to be old, and to have such messes behind you. *The baby born, so beautiful, each tiny finger curled, with the tiny fingernails, and the wisps of blonde hair, and the eyes shut, as if he were only asleep. Can't you do anything? Charles had shouted at the nurses and the doctor. You must be able to do something. Can't you make his heart start beating? And I heard a strange noise,* thought Virginia, *like a terrible laughter, and then I knew it was me, my whole body making the noise, and I could not stop. I shook like a tree in a hurricane, and I said, Let me hold him, and when they had wrapped him in a blanket and I held him, he shook with me, two creatures in a high wind.*

Virginia looked at Charles, standing in the middle of the room. "Could you come sit?"

Charles came and sat on the side of the bed. He pulled her hand into both of his own, and Virginia felt surprised at the warmth and vigor of his touch.

"Feeling better?" Charles asked, his hands making a shell around hers.

"I might be."

"Want some coffee?"

Virginia studied his eyes and his face. He looked quizzical and affectionate. His hair needed cutting, she noted. It waved in small scallops over his ears. His skin had grown more brown and leathery in the sun, with age, but she could still see the line she'd loved, from his forehead to his chin.

"Yes, a cup of coffee might be good."

"I'll make you toast too?"

Virginia thought. She hadn't had an actual breakfast in a long time. "Yes. Toast would be good."

"You'll be all right?"

Charles bent close to her. The question bloomed into the warm air around them.

XIV. Turtle

Early Tuesday afternoon, just after lunch, Sophia Banford pulled the cardboard box around the corner of the house. Turtles liked grass, she thought, and maybe flowers. She liked their sleepy eyelids as they ate. A turtle is funny, how it pulls in its head.

Sophie's mother was in the garden. She looked fat, kneeling by the pink flowers. Her face was pink too, and her hair all messy. She looked like she was thinking.

"Look what I found," said Sophie, pulling the box to her mother.

"Hello, sweetheart," she said. She rubbed her forehead with the back of her hand and made smudges.

"Look what I found," said Sophie.

"A box?"

"A house for a turtle," said Sophie. "I think a turtle will like this house."

Her mother smiled. "Do you have a turtle, Sophie?"

"I'm looking for one," said Sophie. "I think I'll find one in the garden."

Her mother looked funny. "Well," she said. She looked around the garden. "I'm not sure any turtles live here, Sophie."

"How do you know?" Turtles liked grass and flowers. This garden was a good place for turtles. Maybe under the tree. Sophie picked up the box and walked over to the big tree. Under it there was shade and some ivy. Her mother loved ivy. Maybe turtles would hide in ivy.

It was funny about the lady. She was little around her middle, and her hair was pretty, all combed and smooth. When she came this morning, she looked at Sophie like she wanted to hug her. She was talking to her mother, and when Sophie came up she looked like she wanted to hug her. I'm looking for a turtle, Sophie said to her. Would you like a picture of a turtle, she said to Sophie. The lady opened her bag and got a pen. She got a piece of paper. She made a picture of a big turtle on a rock. The turtle winked at Sophie. Do you like it, said the lady. Sophie said yes, only

I wish it was real. The lady laughed. Then Sophie's mother said What a wonderful picture, thank her Sophie, and Sophie said thank you.

Maybe turtles don't like to come out in the day, thought Sophie. Maybe I will wait until after supper, and then I will surprise one back here under the ivy.

And what was her mother talking about with the lady? They bent their heads together and talked so quietly Sophie could not hear. The lady looked a little sad. Maybe a turtle would make her happy. She liked to draw the picture of the turtle. Maybe she would like a real one. They could move fast, and their shells shone like glass when they were wet. They liked water. They could swim in water and stick their necks out just like people.

"Oh, look." Sophie's mother was looking in the flowers.

Sophie ran to her mother.

"Is it a turtle?" she asked.

Her mother shook her head but pointed to a clump of flowers. Sophie looked. Her mother put her finger on her lips and said "Ssh." She pointed. Sophie looked. She saw a bright round thing. It was an eye. The eye blinked. She saw whiskers shaking, and soft fur like gray cotton, all smooth.

"Is it a bunny?" she asked.

Her mother nodded, and the bunny blinked. It had a funny nose, pink and gray.

"Hello bunny," said Sophie.

The bunny looked. Then the flowers shook and the bunny was gone.

"Where did it go?" Sophie sat on her heels. She shaded her eyes to look around the garden.

"Maybe it's hiding," said her mother.

"Maybe it's saying hello to the turtle," said Sophie, and she stood up.

"Maybe so," said her mother. Her mother put her arm around Sophie. She brought her close. She smelled like pancakes.

Sophie put her arms around her mother's neck and pushed her nose into her mother's hair.

"I think bunnies like boxes too," Sophie said.

"I'm sure they do," said her mother, and Sophie patted her mother's head and walked in the hot sun across the garden to find her box in the shade of the big tree.

XV. Phlox

Rose knelt in the grass beside the bed of phlox. The lawn weaving between the flower beds looked straggling, thin and dry in places, and two ant piles made sandy mounds near her knees. The sun, so bright two hours ago, could not be seen now as a distinct thing, for the whole sky had become white and dull. In this light, even the lilies, rich and taut as they were, looked pale. The leaves and stems of the phlox showed the beginnings of a silvery blight.

Today Hallie was leaving. Rose sat back on her heels and pushed her damp hair out of her eyes. Beside her lay a small pile of weeds, the fifth one she had created this afternoon, their roots drying in the heat and their leaves wilting. This bed was beginning to look tended again, the dirt shiny and broken into morsels around the flowers, but what could she do about the phlox? She couldn't remember. Something about the heart of the summer seemed to challenge this garden, to wrest from it all vigor and health.

It looked like rain, Rose thought, as she peered at the sky, grayish-white now, with purple thunderheads rising just over the trees. Rose thought about Hallie's mother. Now that Hallie would be gone, Rose should go see Mrs. Greaves, although the idea made her quail. She couldn't imagine a regular conversation with her, skimming the surface, especially now that Rose knew about her sorrows, and about her attempt to take her own life, but she couldn't imagine a heart-to-heart talk either. Hallie's mother had often had the power to make Rose shiver, she was so cold. I think something's changed for her, Hallie had said this morning. Hallie told Rose how her mother had come outside with her yesterday, and how they had walked along the pool. She'd accepted breakfast and lunch, and had just dozed lightly on the terrace for an hour. She'd stayed outside until dinner, and even after dinner she'd sat with Hallie in the darkening air, listening to the peepers.

Rose felt a sequence of tumblings inside, one after the other, and a little bottom, or a foot, made a sudden bulge just under her breast. Hallie had told Rose how her mother had started to talk about visiting her grandma's house, in Virginia, when she was little. She talked about sitting with her grandma on the porch, Hallie said, how it would be just the two of them, swinging there, with the smell of the barns behind the house, and the sound of crickets. Sometimes she and her grandma heard an owl.

A hush came to the garden. Rose looked at her hands. The dirt had dried, and black lines showed under her fingernails. When she looked up she saw the heavy trees. It was sad about Hallie's baby brother. How could anyone hold such grief inside? Just think, all these years, Hallie could have paid tribute to his memory, somehow. She could have put flowers on the place where he lay, just as she puts flowers on my mother's grave. And I could have known too, Rose thought. I could have offered my tribute too, and Hallie would have had me to share things with.

But as Rose had walked Hallie to her car, Hallie had said, I think I can do it now, I think I can adopt now, with Morey. Rose longed to help with the baby when it came. Why should she and Morey live so far away? How could they live in such a crowded place, anyway, where the air was bad, so far from all this beauty?

Rose sighed. You have to acknowledge, things change, she admonished herself. You might wish everything to stand still, to root itself, but life isn't like that. And William too yearned for change. Just two days ago, at Luke's, where they'd gone for breakfast with Sophie and Elizabeth, he'd talked again about moving, finding a new teaching position somewhere, on one coast or another. Of course his family lived in New Jersey. She could understand the impulse. But (Rose looked at the house, its creamy color, the flower-boxes, Sophie's old trike near the porch, the reflection of sky in the large, calm windows) she couldn't imagine leaving all this, their life here. Her heart seemed all bound up in it, and her writing too.

Rose thought about her characters, hovering near her desk, waiting for their stories to be written, making their quiet and poignant demand. The sky had become gray, and one or two drops of rain touched Rose's nose and her bare shoulder. A memory came to her, of standing on the porch with Hallie one afternoon, as Rose's mother, big-bellied, pregnant, put in bulbs. It had been raining lightly all day, but her mother said the frost was coming soon, and she put on her raincoat and her boots and, as Rose and Hallie watched, she kneeled in the increasing darkness with her trowel and little bags of crocuses and daffodils.

As Rose pulled a couple of weeds, she felt a twinge, long and thin, in her lower back. This is the beginning, she thought in astonishment. It may take four more weeks, but this baby is coming, its presence heralded as if from a distance in the muffled trumpeting of the bundle of muscles at her back. She bent forward, so that her forehead almost brushed against the lavender, as the little trumpet faded. The garden lay around her, the flowers nodding their heads downward as if from too much weight and color. I am not ready, she thought, give me time, although the ache in her flesh, taut and soft, seemed to answer, almost time.

Rose pushed herself slowly up, feeling her knees dirty and crisscrossed by the grass. The rain was coming faster now. She pictured a new title, written in red ink on white paper, something about light, maybe. Her pages, scattered all over her study, seemed to fly together suddenly, assuming shape and form, an airy hall, spacious and yet with alcoves, and doors to other rooms, some of which could only be glimpsed, some of which had to be imagined, like the old Spanish mission she had visited with William, and of course there would be a garden; you would come upon it from various doorways, and each time its color and beauty would sting your eyes.

Rose heard a bumbling noise, a small whirr, and she looked up (one hand on her hip, the other shading her eyes) to see a tiny airplane, a silver pencil high in the sky. It disappeared into the grayness, and Rose walked toward the house, the rain making a fine mist all around her. She pictured herself picking up her red pen and sitting down to begin.

XVI. Wings

Hallie found her seat, over the wing. The plane was almost empty, sunlight coming in on her side so that her seat was bathed in light. She put her bag in the overhead compartment and settled.

After leaving Rose, as she drove with her father to the airport around noon, Hallie had felt a message in the roll of the fields, the light shining on wheat. These smooth rises, this rich color, this meeting of sky and gold, had felt like a letter, or a benediction. Maybe I could paint fields, she had thought with surprise, for never before had this landscape seemed so appealing. I'd have to paint them from memory, though, she had realized, unless I use photographs, and she'd almost asked her father to pull the car over to the side of the road, to wait while she sketched. But the car seemed to fly along, and soon they had reached the airport.

Hallie looked through her little window at the airport building. The sky had grown suddenly cloudy. Purple clouds loomed on the horizon, and pale gray ones sat plumply overhead. A drop of rain made a tiny stream on the glass. Had he left? or was he standing inside, waiting until her plane lifted into the sky? He would go home then, and roll the car into the driveway, and hear the sound of his shoes on the gravel. And what would happen then? wondered Hallie, picturing her wish, that her mother would come downstairs to greet him, and that they could sit together, as they must have done once, talking, and not worrying about the rain pelting the driveway and the garden, and making a little sea out of the swimming pool.

The plane backed up, and moved along the runway, slowly, and then faster. Hallie felt the plane lumber into the air. The runway raced by beneath and the fields offered themselves quickly to her sight as rectangles and squares of color: yellow, green, gold. Suddenly Ohio looked small. Wisps of clouds spread beneath the airplane, making the landscape misty.

On Sunday she had followed her father into the solarium, and as he watered his ferns and jades, and a little orange tree with small white blossoms glancing through the branches, she had gotten up the courage to ask some of the questions rising in her. What happened to the baby? was her first one, and her father had put down the watering-can and looked out the window. He had not seemed able to answer, so Hallie had asked, Did you bury him? Her father had nodded. Close by? He nodded again. You mean, in the cemetery? How terrible, she had thought, all these years she'd grieved for Rose's mother, lying there on the hillside, and her brother had been not even a dot on her horizon.

Hallie had asked to see the grave, and her father had at first tried to put her off—it would upset her mother, he said, better to wait until her next visit—but she had pressed him, and after awhile he agreed to take her there. As the car backed out of the driveway, her mother had come out of the house. Where are you going? she asked, and her father had said, Just downtown. Where, downtown? And her father had looked at the steering wheel. Her mother must have known this was coming. She had stood by the car. I'm coming too, she had said then, and Hallie, amazed, had jumped out to give her mother the front seat. They had made the silent journey downtown, past May's street, and past the college, along Broadway almost to Rose's house, turning down Cherry and then into the cemetery between the old stone gates.

At the cemetery, though, her mother had stayed in the car. Hallie had walked with her father up the slope to a corner of the cemetery she had never noticed. A small tree with long trailing fronds stood gracefully in an expanse of rough grass. Nearby, a small stone, placed flat on the ground, said James Holloway Greaves, Beloved Son of Virginia and Charles Greaves. Charles bent to pull at the shaggy grass around it. Until that moment, Hallie had not thought about the baby as having a name.

Hallie looked up to see a stewardess standing in the aisle, staring at her. She had dyed blonde hair, the brown roots showing by an inch, and violet eyeshadow. She had plucked her eyebrows a few days ago, the little hairs making their way back, for a ragged effect.

"What can I get you to drink?"

Hallie glanced at the cans of soda. "Do you have cranberry juice?"

The woman bent to find it, a slight scowl on her face. She popped the can open and poured the red liquid into a plastic cup, handing it to Hallie with a little pack of peanuts.

Want a magazine? her father had asked right before Hallie had boarded, looking around the airport as if eager to offer her something. No, thanks, she had said. A book? How about a book? No, thanks, I'm in the middle of one at home, I just forgot to bring it with me. Well, you could have one to tide you over, he'd suggested, but she'd said, I think I'll just do some sketching on the plane. Well, Hal, he had said, and his eyes had seemed to search her face. Will Morey be meeting you? Yes. Any plans for the summer? We might go up to Connecticut, for a week, in August, Hallie had said. A look of sadness had shadowed her father's face then. But he had put his hand into his pocket, and said, Oh, I almost forgot. I got this for you. For the plane. He held out an Almond Joy. Hallie had laughed, and thanked him, and in the next breath she had felt overcome. It's not much, he said. It's fine, it's perfect, and for a moment the Almond Joy seemed to mark the bridge between them, paper and chocolate, a kind of fragility and sweetness. I hope you're all right, he had said then. All right? Yes, of course I'm all right. Say hello to Morey. I will. The voice on the loudspeaker had called for boarding children and passengers needing special assistance, and in another moment Hallie's section was called. Goodbye, she had said, bringing her face near. He kissed her on the forehead. I'll come home again soon, she had said. He had nodded, and waved.

Hallie looked out the window. Outside all was white, but she pictured her parents' house, the wild cherries scattered across the lawn and the pool, and she pictured too the quiet green slope graced by a small tree. Goodbye, she said under her breath, as the plane rose above an ocean of whiteness that stretched to the horizon. She could see the shadow of the plane, bluish gray, moving across it. The sky, above these clouds, glowed a splendid blue. Such lucidity up here, thought Hallie. Blue air like this could clear out your mind in seconds, and she imagined a golden broom, one an angel would use, sweeping the hall of her mind, opening all her drawers and her portfolios and tossing out her old sketches, one by one, so that the paper fluttered miles to the ground, and poking the broom into the arches to sweep away the dust and old birds' nests. A good mid-summer cleaning, the angel said, that's what you need; we'll have you good as new in a jiffy. An optimistic and industrious angel. How lovely to look at the hall broom-clean. You could walk up and down, looking out at sky, and see polished floors, clear of furniture, and open windows.

Into this hall Hallie envisioned something on the wing—a stork, was it? or a pelican? She saw herself catching a bundle as the bird tossed it to her: a baby. She would keep it safe from all the sorrows of the world.

The cloud ocean had moved up to the airplane somehow, and soon wisps of mist threaded by, and then the plane seemed to plunge into the clouds so that all was white, with silvery tinges. The whiteness mingled with a jumble of images: her mother's hands, her father's kiss, the small gray stone, the little girl counting fish at the hospital, Rose's belly on the diamond-patterned blanket, Sophie pointing to her turtle box. I should open my sketchbook, thought Hallie, but she felt drowsy. As she drifted into sleep, she thought she could hear a voice calling to her, but she could not distinguish the words from the drone of the plane and her memory of seagulls crying as they whirled overhead.

In her dream, she stood in an art gallery showing slides of her paintings to a man with a shock of white hair and a blue tie. She felt surprised, because each slide she showed him was new to her: three large canvases of glittering wings, burnished gold but with threads of crimson woven in with other colors. Suddenly she was in the street. A girl stood by a bicycle. It was Rose, and she put her hand into

Hallie's. We have to get home, she said, and Hallie got on the back of the bicycle and together they rode through streets crowded with people and cars. Rose's red hair blew into Hallie's face as Hallie put her arms around her waist and watched the sidewalk skim by.

When Hallie opened her eyes, she looked out the window to see a city below, and soon she could see the airport. The clouds now hung overhead in a thick mass, making the sky look pale. Landing, the plane bumped twice, and then slowed. Hallie took out her brush and her lipstick, peering at herself in the little mirror. She brushed her hair hard. Morey would be here, she knew, hanging back a little way behind the crowd, waiting to embrace her. All around her people rose, reaching into the overhead compartments and bending to pull briefcases and purses from under seats. On the window drops of rain dashed, making tiny silver hieroglyphs. As she put on her lipstick, and then gathered up her bag, she felt Rose's hair on her face and saw her own feet held above the pavement as the bicycle flew on.